Catri

Thank you

x

Bradd Chambers

daddy's
little
girl

Bradd Chambers

Bradd Chambers

Other publications from Bradd Chambers:

'Someone Else's Life'
Released June 2017
Available now on Amazon

'Our Jilly'
Released November 2017
Available now on Amazon

'In Too Deep'
Released February 2019
Available now on Amazon

Bradd Chambers

Daddy's Little Girl

Readers are loving books by Bradd Chambers.

Praise for *'Someone Else's Life:'*

"*With this dark, gritty debut, Bradd Chambers marks himself out as one to watch in crime writing.*"
Brian McGilloway.

'*Enthralling,*' '*Awesome*' and '*Would make a great movie.*' '*A book for every thriller novel lover.*'
MCXV Reviewer.

"*A great first novel by Bradd Chambers, very well written with an enticing storyline and I was shocked when I found out the killer. Was certainly kept guessing until the end. Excellent read.*"
Amazon Reviewer.

"*This was a great read, snappy chapters, good style of writing, avoided being unnecessarily graphic in the murder scenes, interesting characters and kept me guessing to the end. My kind of crime thriller, really enjoyed.*"
Goodreads Reviewer.

Bradd Chambers

Praise for *'Our Jilly:'*

"Brilliant book. I was hooked from the first page, truly would be a fantastic gift for the Sherlock in your life."
Amazon Reviewer.

"This is the second book I have read by this author and was not disappointed! Could not put the book down and read it all in a day, [I'm] looking forward to reading more from this author and would 100% recommend this book to anyone looking for [a] great read!"
Goodreads Reviewer.

"Another 5-star book from this stand-alone author, and again I would highly recommend. As a fan of murder mystery, I still thoroughly enjoyed this book despite the reveal of the murderer from the offset. You will turn each page craving justice for Jilly wondering will the murderer get away with it!"
Amazon Reviewer.

"The second book I've read by Bradd - both are completely captivating stories that make it near impossible to stop turning the pages! Absolutely brilliant read, can't wait for the next book by this author."
Amazon Reviewer.

Praise for *'In Too Deep:'*

"This is the first book I've read by Bradd but won't be the last. It was well written with solid believable characters. It tackles issues such as suicide and mental health issues in a very real way. I read this book in just one sitting as I was enthralled with the main characters and couldn't put it down. I would thoroughly recommend this book to everyone."
Goodreads Reviewer.

"A very clever thriller with many twists and turns through its entirety. I really enjoyed this book. Well worth a read."
Amazon Reviewer.

"Thoroughly enjoyed this book. I was gripped from the first chapter and just could not put it down. The plot was clever and every twist had me hooked. The book has a large focus on mental health and suicide, particularly in Londonderry, with the main character running a charity and running campaigns to help raise money and awareness to help [the] prevent[ion] of suicide. Massive praise for Bradd for writing about such a difficult subject and for helping to raise awareness himself. Please read this book! Highly recommended."
Goodreads Reviewer.

Bradd Chambers

Daddy's Little Girl

For all the people that made my time
at university the best years of my life.
*(Look out for the Easter eggs of your
names in some of my characters)*.

Bradd Chambers

Daddy's Little Girl

And for Liverpool,
the city I fell in love with.

Bradd Chambers

Chapter One:

The hot air dial has reached its limit and will no longer turn clockwise as the old machine bursts to life, instantly coming to war with the condensation enveloping the windscreen. I watch as it evaporates, slowly moving up the window until I can see the entrance to the bar perfectly. The doormen are still checking people's IDs and chatting amongst themselves, stamping their feet and rubbing their hands to keep warm. They haven't noticed that I'm here... Waiting... They needn't worry. It's not them I'm here for.

I'm sitting in the car park on the crossroads between Seel Street and Slater Street, after following his taxi from a party in Smithdown. He blundered out of it and had a mini-argument with the bald bouncer to prove his sobriety, before being ushered in out of the cold. He hadn't even bothered to bring a jacket, but I guess very little people on the streets do these days. Their young skin thickened by the effects of alcohol and drugs.

I remember the last time I was around these parts at this time of night. Malcolm had been back for the weekend, and of course he wouldn't let me say no to a few cold ones down at our old local, the Blue Angel. We had proceeded down this very street towards the Novotel, and although a short walk of no more than a few minutes, we were shocked to be approached by two different men asking us if we needed any *'Charlie'* or *'Molly.'* Not as hip and down with the kids as I am, I had to translate the drug nicknames to my oldest school friend, who had been shocked that they were so easily accessible.

"Too accessible," I say out loud, turning down the dial a smidge as sweat starts to stick my shirt to my back.

The boy had almost spotted me when he dodged across the road during the party to scrabble into a neighbouring car. Shrunken in my own vehicle to avoid being seen, I hadn't observed much of what went on, but I got the gist of the meeting... He had bought drugs. The slam of the door echoed through Cumberland Avenue as he ran back into his party and the blacked-out car had sped off, tyres screeching towards the direction of Sefton Park. He had definitely seemed a lot more animated once he left an hour later.

Now, all I have to do is wait...

Chapter Two:

"Oi, mate. You got some on my new fucking trainees!"

Lee burps sluggishly and lags his head backwards until he's staring up at the dimly lit ceiling. He can just about make out the outline of another boy backing away from him. Slumping indolently onto his knees and resting his throbbing head against the cracked tiles behind, his eyes roll in his head and he urges the room to stop spinning. He feels the floor swing to his left like he's inside a washing machine on an extra dry cycle and tries desperately to focus on gravity weighing his body to the piss-soaked bathroom floor, the vibrations from the music not helping. After a few moments, he hiccups and vomit splutters from his mouth once more, inept of any movement or he'd manoeuvre his neck inches to his right, so it could spill into the already overflowing urinal.

Once the wave of nausea has subsided, he opens one eye to see that he's finally alone, bar the signature foreign toilet attendant, who flashes him his widest grin.

"Okay, my friend?"

Lee burps again before levering himself up off the undulate floor by grasping onto the pipes connecting the urinals. Once on his feet, he lumbers over to the sink and looks himself in the mirror. Fuck, he looks rough. He has to close one eye to focus on the blurred outline in front of him, swaying back and forth with sick all down his new shirt. The attendant starts frantically brushing the harsh green paper down his front and sprays him with Lynx. Leading Lee by the arm closer to the sink, he splashes warm water and soap onto his hands, before pushing out a piece of chewing gum from his crinkled packet. Proud of his accomplishment, he beams at Lee once more.

"Good as new, my friend."

Lee smiles sheepishly, his eyes still not being able to focus. Bringing out his wallet, coins spill from his pocket and skirt around the room. As the attendant hastily proceeds to gather them, Lee decides that that will be sufficient payment and pulls open the door, the sound of the new Calvin Harris song and the strobe lights greeting him.

Chapter Three:

A half hour later, Lee is roaring and screaming as his legs frail around in the air. Two of the doormen grabbing an arm either side and hoisting him up so he can't drag his feet. Out into the cold air and down three steps, they drop Lee to the ground.

"The fuck you playin' at, mate?" he spits at them.

He remembers the bald one from earlier, scowling at his ID and asking him what star sign he was. Stating he was too drunk when Lee informed him he didn't believe in any of that shit.

"Empty your pockets."

"Fuck you!"

"Empty your pockets or we're calling the bizzies," the bald man's eyes glare into Lee's, struggling to find the colour behind the dark bulging pupils.

Lee mumbles something incomprehensible before turning out his pockets, his phone and wallet falling to the ground with two sharp slaps. The doorman reaches for Lee's wallet, a cheap leather bound with an Everton Football Club band wrapped around it to stop the contents from spilling out. The wallet produces nothing but a student card from the local college and a handful of silver change.

"Fuck you want my wallet for?"

"Want to see what you've been using to snort up your Charlie."

"I ain't been taking no Charlie," Lee growls, the debit card in his back pocket suddenly becoming that much heavier.

"Don't lie to us."

"Fuckin' not," Lee snatches the wallet back and trips across the road, giving the doorman the fingers before sulking off around the corner and out of sight.

Chapter Four:

As he staggers towards the city centre, I lurch the car into gear and spin after him. He roams aimlessly between buildings and streets, making it hard to follow with the persistent drunk people and one-way systems. I lose him a few times, just to find him again moments later. Does he have no direction? What is his motive?

Finally, after a quarter of an hour of traipsing about, I sigh and pull up the handbrake gratefully as I watch as he skips the queue in the Subway. He starts gesturing frantically to the sandwich-maker on the other side of the station, a young Asian woman who looks frightened and out of her depth. After a few moments, a bloke in the queue gets involved. An argument ensues, leaving me to try and lip-read as they physically wave their hands at one another.

It's when another lad steps in that my target launches himself forward, fists first. Of course, with him being off his face, I'm not surprised that he's no Rocky Balboa. His fist misses the second lad,

23

bouncing off the glass window. Creasing his face up in pain and hugging his injured wrist against his chest with his free hand, he receives a blow from behind from the first guy. Despite the hum of the old engine, the blowing of the heating system and the inches of glass, I can still hear the screams of the sandwich-maker, bellowing at them to get out.

Barrelling out onto the street, the two lads force him onto the ground and start kicking him in the stomach. Despite being at a disastrous disadvantage, he still tries to climb back onto his feet. I can hear the curses and threats that he throws at his aggressors. Saying that he'll get them and calling them a bunch of scallies.

Finally, he lies down and admits defeat. The two lads nod to one another sullenly, their temporary alliance broken. One swings the door of the fast food franchise open whilst the other wraps his arms around his girl and slogs off, spitting on him as they pass.

After he is convinced he can get up without being attacked again, or after he regains consciousness, I'm unsure, he wobbles himself back towards the direction he came in. I follow at a snail's pace, keeping my distance, aware of anything that might incriminate me, despite the stolen car. He attempts to thumb down pre-booked Ubers, full taxis or random cars, getting that little bit more discouraged every time they honk at him to get off the road, or whizz past carelessly.

I decide now is as good of a chance as any, and rev my engine to announce my phoney arrival. He's walking up a side street I've never been down before, but with no businesses, cameras or onlookers, it's like he's walked straight into my trap. The lights of the car flood him as his head turns towards the source, tottering cautiously to one side, in danger of falling over. He steps onto the pavement and strides on, dragging his left side along the wall. Maybe he isn't as vulnerable and desperate as I thought? I get an idea. Pulling up and rolling down the window, I bark out to him.

"Er... Reid?"

The first surname that pops into my head. His eyes focus on me as he steps away from the wall.

"You what, mate?"

"Cab for Reid?"

He scrunches up his face before cogs start to turn in his inebriated brain.

"Yeah, yeah... Reid."

And with that, he hops into my back seat and I speed off before anyone has the chance to see. As I pull onto Duke Street, I steal a glimpse of him in the rear-view mirror. His head is swaying from side to side, blood and sick down his front. Then I remember an important detail of my role.

"Where ya going, pal?" I cough.

He lolls his head backwards and looks at my reflection with a tiny gap between his eyes.

"Widnes," he whispers, before closing his eyes fully again and dropping his chin to connect with his chest.

"Right you are," I smile, "just gonna take the long road around here, the streets are carnage at the minute."

I needn't have bothered, he's already out for the count. No clue that instead of going west, I'm heading straight up north. To my carefully selected spot where there will be no interruptions, no intruders and no one to hear his screams.

Chapter Five:

Jerking awake, Lee has a mini panic attack as he's caught by the seatbelt, pulling him back into place. He frails around him, eyes wild and scrabbles about for any familiarity.

"You alright, kid?"

Registering the voice and letting his eyes adjust, Lee sees a man in the front seat of the car turning around and flashing him a grin. Embarrassed, he attempts to settle himself, willing his heart to do the same. When his breathing returns to normal, he tries to remember how he got here. Racking his brain to think about where he was or what he was doing before getting into a car with a stranger, who he can only assume is a taxi driver.

Distorted memories start to creep back into his brain like vines in a horror movie. He remembers the club... The dealer... The toilets... Everything's a blur. But how did he end up here? Perching himself in a more comfortable position in the backseat, he gazes out of the window to be met with nothing but dark fields. Confused, he turns to his supposed saviour.

"Er... Sorry. But where are we exactly?"

"Nearly there."

The driver doesn't bother to turn his head this time. Nearly where? Lee thinks.

"Sorry, a little flaky on what's happened. Where are we going?"

The driver looks into the rear-view mirror and smirks.

"Rough night?"

"I guess you could say that... Maybe."

"You were looking a little rough when I found you."

"Found me?"

"Yeah, I had just had a drop off outside the Tesco on Bold Street when I saw you stumbling about. Had got a right old beatin' outside the Subway."

"Subway..." Lee whispers.

He places a hand to his head to feel it crusty with dried blood. He had assumed the pounding head and sores all over his body to be some sort of come down.

"So," the man continues, "I thought I'd pick you up and take you home before you got yourself into anymore trouble."

Lee's glad it's dark so the driver can't see his blush.

"Thanks, mate. But... Where are we?"

"Like I said, nearly there."

"I don't recognise this way."

Turning around once again, the driver winks.

"Shortcut."

Chapter Six:

Five more minutes pass with nothing of significance to view on our voyage, making it easier for me, as I turn down the same country road for the fourth time. I thought he'd nod off to sleep, or maybe conk out from the chemicals again, but my little troublemaker seems to be adamant to stay conscious until he's safely back home.

I must think of something. And quickly. He's already suspicious, and with every passing moment the feeling will grow stronger until I'll have to answer questions I don't have the answers to. My brain whirls in my head, thinking over different scenarios and weighing their credibility. Until finally...

Indicating left and pulling into a layby, I can sense him shuffling uncomfortably behind me. Bringing my phone from my jacket, I press the voicemail button secretively.

"Where are w-"

"Sorry, mate. Won't be long. Got to take this. Office calling."

Pressing the phone to my ear, I'm greeted with Benny's laughing voice. I step out of the car and slam the door, apologising loudly as I trudge off into the darkness. When I'm a safe distance away and satisfied he can no longer see me, I start to jog uphill towards the farm. The night is even colder out here without the glare from the city lights, and my lungs feel frozen with each intake of breath.

Finally, when it starts to physically hurt to breathe, I see the old abandoned well. The redbrick coated in moss, but still a welcome sight regardless. Tapping it as I pass, I walk the fifty feet up the dirt track and turn the corner to meet the old buildings head on. I put all my strength into my shoulder as I push through into the resilient shed. Switching my phone's torch app on, I find it difficult to decide which of my beautiful equipment I should present to my new plaything.

Chapter Seven:

Twisting in the seat precariously until his neck gets sore, Lee decides to unlock himself from his belt restraint. He turns his body around until his knees dig into the cheap leather and presses his face against the back window, hands engulfing his temples to shelter any of the unnecessary landscapes from view. But he still can't find the man. This definitely is starting to feel like something from the movies. The driver steps out for a second to take a quick phone call and ends up dead in the dirt with his throat slit. Lee helplessly waiting to be the psychopath's next victim.

He physically shakes his head, like that will help the thoughts tumble out of his brain. He's watched too much TV, and the paranoia from the drugs isn't helping. Nick said this could happen. He sits back the right way around again and exhales. Seconds later, he jumps with fright as a sharp clicking sound echoes around the car. He almost chuckles audibly as he glares again out of the window, convinced that the sound has come from the taxi man's return, pressing his keys to unlock his car out of habit. But still no sign of life.

Gazing out across the fields, the only lights he can see are from buildings he guesses are miles and miles away. Getting impatient, he reaches for the handle of the door, deciding that his senses will heighten against danger if he can at least stand outside and have the slightest chance of escape. But the handle won't budge. After forcing all his weight upon it, he shuffles over to the alternative, but is met with the same problem. Bloody child locks. He starts to panic after clambering into the front seats to try their doors. He sits midway in the vehicle, breathing heavily and forces his head into his knees until he sees colours dancing around inside his head. That sound wasn't the taxi man unlocking the doors, it was the car automatically locking him in!

"Focus, Lee, focus," he snaps to himself, claustrophobia heightening as the car seems to shrink a few sizes.

Scrambling around the vehicle in the dark, he finds nothing but empty sweet wrappers. Where the fuck is his phone? Pulling out the glove compartment, he's met with an old mouldy car air freshener in the shape of a tree and an out of date MOT certificate addressed to a Grace Kirkwood. The driver's wife? His eyes immediately jerk to above the dashboard, but he can't see any form of identification for his taxi driver. Not even so much as a GPS system or phone holder.

"Shit!"

Kicking with all his strength at the windows and doors, he exhausts himself quickly, melting onto the back seat and trembling with whimpers. Opening his eyes, he sees the stars above him and wonders if this is the last time he'll see them.

"The stars!" he shouts, elevating himself so his feet are in the air once more.

He starts kicking repeatedly and desperately at the sunroof, willing it to give way. Moments later, he's finally greeted with a spray of glass and a deafening smash. Sheltering his face with his arms from the majority of the fallen debris, he climbs up on his elbows, ready to clamber out to safety. But he hasn't broken through the sunroof at all. It's still very much intact.

A dry chuckle comes from behind him and he spins around to see the back-passenger side window agape, bits of glass still blistering out from the sides like a broken television screen. And tonight's movie? His abductor standing with the same grin on his face, one hand wrapped around a black metal rod, his other inching closer to the door handle.

Chapter Eight:

Trying to fight your way through the hustle and bustle of Brown's Market & Shopping Centre is hard enough on a drizzly Wednesday morning without the added congestion of officers and onlookers. DI Atkins and DS Parkes struggle to stick to each other's sides as they battle towards the exit onto Houghton Street, bypassing all walks of life trying to get themselves the best deals in Liverpool City.

Safely in the car, they rev the engine and flash their emergency lights to bully the pedestrians out of their way, before pulling into Houghton Lane and parking up again. This side street is rarely used by shoppers due to the secluded shutters and mossy pavements. Perfect privacy for a homeless man, or drunk student, to take a piss undetected. Or, in this case, two detectives wanting to get their nicotine fix before their return to the station.

"Do you not miss it?" Atkins smirks at Parkes, not bothering to blow the smoke out of the open window and watching as it momentarily obstructs his partner's face.

"Nope, not since this little beauty," she beams, brandishing the e-cig in front of her before taking a long drag.

Atkins grimaces as his own cigarette smell is overpowered with the flowery stink of her vape.

"Yuck, what's it today? Dandelions? Daisies?"

Parkes chuckles.

"Trifle."

Atkins gags for the second time in minutes, the prior retch accumulating from the rancid fumes from the fish aisle in the market. His stomach still hasn't settled properly. He'd need a Maccies to keep him going today.

After Parkes's giggles have subsided, she pockets the vape and looks in the rear-view mirror at the passing shoppers and the looming Greggs sign. She still hasn't touched a cup of coffee since finding out she was pregnant with Josh. Now he's a bright and bouncing one-year-old, and she hasn't felt the need to go back to her dark habit. But cigarettes? Adjusting to vapes was hard enough after hopelessly trying to cut out on nicotine completely. She just wishes she had've been able to quit, even just for those few months, for Josh's sake more than her own.

These thoughts remind her of nestling out her back garden behind a bin, even when she was so heavily pregnant she couldn't bend. Hormones driving her looney as she chugged desperately on her e-cig, hoping that no neighbours, family members or even Callum would catch her. She told them all she was trying everything she could, which wasn't a lie. It wasn't her fault that the patches and gum were apathetic to her changing body.

"So," Atkins sighs after stubbing out his cigarette, wrapping it in a tissue and pocketing it, "Alvi?"

Parkes splutters.

"Full of it."

They had been called out to the precinct first thing this morning after a customer had bought a suitcase from Iskandar Bargains, only to find the insides lined with bags of cocaine. After just speaking with Behram Alvi, the store owner, they suspect that this activity has been going on for some time, notwithstanding Alvi's protested innocence and oblivion.

"My father opened this business, this *respected* business, forty years ago. Forty years, we've been serving the people of this city. We are not criminals. We give the people of Liverpool what they want. Bargains. Not drugs," he had assured the detectives, before being escorted off the premises by uniformed officers.

Despite his thought provoking speech, SOCOs had found several similar suitcases only just delivered at 6am this morning, with a few pounds additionally shoved effortlessly in a locked cupboard, sniffed out by Ben, the newly trained drug hound.

"Looks like he could be going down for quite some time."

Atkins shakes his head as he crawls the vehicle through the main shopping streets of Liverpool One, before turning right onto Hanover Street and towards the station by the famous docks. As the pair come to a stop in front of yet another set of traffic lights, Atkins's phone blares on the handsfree.

"Amanda, how are you?"

"Sound. You still got a cob on?"

Atkins shifts uncomfortably in the driver seat, flashing Parkes a hearty grin.

"No, no. Just had a bit of a headache."

"A headache? You looked a right mess when I saw ya this morning."

"Fine, Mand. Didn't get much sleep last night, is all."

Amanda laughs over the phone, making her modicum of bangles jingle distractively near the handset.

"How was Brown's, then?"

"Iskandar Bargains is on a total shut down. We should have Alvi already waiting in the station and his staff are currently getting questioned. A few SOCOs still poking around the place. Dotting the i's and all that."

"So, you're finished?"

"Yeah, Parkes and I are heading back now. Probably be another ten minutes."

"Well, that's why I'm ringing. We've got a Marie Wright in with us. Said her son's missing. Went on a night out and never came home. You wouldn't sort this out for us?"

Atkins groans and looks at Parkes helplessly, but she looks concerned.

"I'll see you when I see you. Won't be long."

"Thanks, boss. Ta-ra."

He presses the red button to hang up and pulls onto Strand Street, flying past cars towards the station.

"Why aren't you more worried about this?" Parkes eyes her superior suspiciously.

Atkins grips the steering wheel attentively, wanting the pounding in his head to go away.

"You see cases like this all the time. You know nothing ever comes of it. Just another student on a mad one and never told their worried mam."

"That's not always the case, sir. What about the girl who committed suicide last year, or the body found in the Mersey? You shouldn't write someone off before you get all the information."

Atkins brakes at another red light and blows out in thought.

"You're right, Parkes. I'm sorry. Just not feeling myself today."

She nods and resumes her attention to the passenger-side window, despite looking like she wants to say a lot more as he pushes the car into gear and heads towards the latest problem looming over their heads.

Chapter Nine:

The reception is filled with the echoes of Marie's sobbing, leaving the detectives to throw Amanda a courteous smile, their unasked question of her whereabouts answered, before clambering into the small waiting room. Two orange sofas take up the majority of the space, with a sad looking plant wedged between them. Marie looks up from her stained used hankie and wrinkles her eyes at the sight of them, trying to quash her tears. The large lady engulfs much of the sofa furthest from the door, as she indents the cushions by nestling in the centre. Her blue flower designed dress is shrouded in a charred black cardigan which strains around her shoulders. Her hair is greasy and hangs to the side of her wet face. She snorts as she stands, the sofa groaning with relief beneath her.

"You who I need to speak to?" she bellows.

"Yes, Mrs Wright," Parkes crosses the small round rug to greet her. "Please, sit, sit."

Parkes encourages Marie back down onto the sofa, melting back into her original groove while the sergeant perches awkwardly on the arm.

"It's Lee. He's missing."

Atkins falls gracelessly into the neighbouring settee, cursing the bright lights above their heads and the heat of the enclosed room.

"Please, Mrs Wright, can y-" Atkins begins.

"It's not '*Mrs.*' I'm no longer married."

"Sorry, Miss..."

"Wright."

"Right."

Atkins steals an agitated glance at Parkes as Marie buries her face in the handkerchief again, but Parkes is rubbing the lady's huge hand reassuringly.

"When's the last time you saw Lee?"

"Last night. He was comin' up here with his mates."

"Up here?"

"Yeah, we live in Widnes."

"Does he come up often?"

"Yeah, he goes to college in the city so most of his friends live around here."

"And has he never stayed over at any of their houses... Anything like that?"

"No, never. He hates it. Likes to come home to his own bed and a bacon sarnie the next morning. He's never done anything like this before."

"Could there be a girlfriend on the scene? Maybe he's stayed at hers?"

Marie's head snaps towards Atkins as if he had suggested something completely ludicrous and out of the question.

"No, of course not. He'd tell his mam. He tells me everything."

The two detectives give each other a side glance whilst the woman blows her nose. They both know that's not true, both as parents and officers of the law.

"Have you tried calling him?" Parkes takes over again.

"Of course I have. It just goes straight to voicemail."

"Have you tried anyone he was out with?"

"No, I'm not in the town much. Only for Christmas presents and that. I've never met any of them."

"He hasn't brought anyone back to the house or..."

"No, never."

"What about his dad?"

Her eyes bulge in disgust again.

"His dad doesn't give a crap about him."

"Is he... In the picture?"

"God, no. Hasn't been since he was six-years-old."

"Is there a chance he could have gone to see him?"

"Well, I very much doubt so. He lives in Spain."

"And there's been no contact whatsoever?"

"No, not really. Well... That I know of... But like I said, he'd tell his mam. I'm all he's got. That good-for-nothing bastard would hardly ever even call me back when he was a little'un. We went through the courts 'cause I wanted him to have nothing to do with Lee. Then, when he was allowed a few hours on a Saturday, he shipped off with some slag to Spain. Sends him a birthday and Christmas card with a few Euro notes in 'em twice a year. That's nice of him," she spits sarcastically.

"Okay, should you contact him, just in case?"

"Will I hell. Haven't spoken to the man in over ten years."

"Did Lee mention who he was going out with?" Parkes takes over again, trying to get the woman back onside.

"Todd... Something. That's all I can remember, sorry."

"It's okay, please try and remember anything."

The lady's weeps halt as she points a finger accusatorily towards Atkins.

"Oh... He said something about a party."

"Maybe he's still there?"

"No, no. He was going there before."

"Before?"

"Before going out into town."

"Does he have class on Wednesdays, maybe you missed him?" Atkins stares lazily at the dehydrated plant, not sure if he supressed the sigh as he spoke.

"No, definitely not. Wednesdays are their days off, that's why they always go to that place on a Tuesday night."

"That place?" Parkes nods.

It feels like they're getting somewhere through the lady's hysteria.

"Yeah, that club. Oh... What's it called? What's it called? Juicy or delish or something."

"Tasty?" Atkins suggests, ignoring the raise in one of Parkes's eyebrows as she glances towards him.

"Yeah, that one. He was there," Marie's eyes engulf her head.

Tasty isn't the name of a club, but a promo night in Bangers Bar on Slater Street. Students flock there on weekdays for cheap booze and popular music.

"Right, well that's as good of a place to start as any," Atkins slaps his knees as he stands.

"Please find him," Marie grabs Atkins's wrist.

"We'll try everything we can," he smiles at her through his disgust, both at her snotty nose and the churning in his stomach.

After delegating the investigation of the cocaine raid on Iskandar Bargains with another department for the time being, the two detectives are in the car speeding off towards town once more.

"Tasty?" Parkes smirks.

"Yeah, don't remind me," Atkins laughs.

"Bit young for you, that crowd, don't you think?"

Atkins manages a chuckle.

"Olivia has been badgering me about it. Her friend goes with her sister sometimes."

"Underage drinking, and on a school night and everything? She has some nerve," Parkes smiles before returning her attention to the passenger-side window.

Atkins glances sideways towards her momentarily before his eyes glaze over.

"Yeah... Some nerve."

Chapter Ten:

Parking up outside a kebab takeaway, Atkins and Parkes slam their car doors, the sound echoing through the still hungover cobbles. It's hard to believe that less than 12 hours ago these streets in the middle of Liverpool's infamous party scene were packed with revellers, music, laughter and fights. Now, in the dull light of day, there is nothing left but the odd pool of sick to indicate that this is arguably one of the best places to flock to in the UK.

Crossing the forsaken road, the detectives step into the heat of Bangers Bar. They're met with light music and a lounge area, with wafts of burgers coming from the kitchen to their left. Their heavy feet thud across the wooden floor as they dodge past the sparsely placed leather sofas and wooden benches before they spot the long bar on the right. There, they see a young blonde girl with her face buried in a textbook. Looking up with a warm smile, she hops off her stool and pods over, barely reaching the taps of the impressive selection of ale the business offers.

"Hiya hon, what can I get ya?"

After introducing themselves, the girl looks a lot more nervous.

"We're actually here to see if we can speak to someone about a missing person. He's believed to have attended your student night last night."

The girl nods, biting her lip.

"Afraid I wasn't working last night. But I can find you someone who was?"

"Thank you."

She shuffles off and leaves the detectives to glance around the room in her wake. Scoping out the scene. Parkes turns around to see Atkins observing the drink taps in front of the bar.

"Sir?"

"Never been here before, nice place. Food smells great."

Parkes raises an eyebrow before smiling towards the girl on her return.

"I'm sorry, but everyone's day staff here. My boss says that Lenny will be in in a half hour though."

"Lenny?"

"Yeah, he's the doorman. Has worked here years and years. He was on the late last night. Want me to grab you something while you wait?"

Parkes opens her mouth to protest, but is

shocked to see Atkins melt into one of the leather sofas.

"Yes, thanks. That would be great. Grab me a Brewdog and a..." he elongates the last word as he lifts a corner of the menu. "A double cheese burger. Ta, love."

The girl beams at him before jerking her body towards Parkes.

"Er... I'll have an orange juice."

"And food?"

Parkes's eyes return to her superior.

"She said he'll be a half hour," he shrugs.

Pursing her lips, she sighs.

"I'll just have a plate of chicken wings, please."

Nodding gratefully, the girl turns to leave.

"Does the burger come with chips?"

Chapter Eleven:

She always loved bowling. Ever since that first time I took her when her mam was hungover that Father's Day. She must've just been shy of five-years-old. She wanted the purple ball, of course. But it was too heavy. She wasn't happy and pulled a strop, not wanting the orange extra-light one. So, using the ramp, I helped her throw the purple one, which was even too heavy for me. The ball bounced from the bumpers at the sides of the lane and knocked out eight skittles. She couldn't have been happier with herself, jumping up and down with glee and cheering with a huge grin. It made me laugh how something so simple could bring such joy to her little face. I let her win... That time.

We got nuggets and chips from the Maccies across the carpark afterwards. I can still remember her trying to work out how the toy from her Happy Meal worked. That cute little confused look reserved for adult activities she refused to let us complete. The tip of her tongue stuck out to the side as she tried to fit together the awkward pieces.

That's the day we got those matching keyrings. Some cheap stupid pieces of metal from a discount retail store that went on to mean so much. Two pieces of a broken heart that fit together to make a whole one. *'I love u'* inscribed on each one. I still remember her face as she marched over with them in her clammy hand. Seeing her tongue wiggle through her missing front teeth.

"That way we'll always be together, even when you're in work and I'm in school. Right daddy?"

That day became something of a father-daughter tradition. Once every few weeks, usually when her mother was hungover, we'd go and enjoy ourselves. Angela would never want to join, just shrugging off our attempts and pulling the duvet over her head. Her mother's protests used to dishearten her, until she just never bothered asking her anymore. In fact, in my own selfish way, I was glad of the time alone together. Work was getting more stressful, and I was missing out on plays and sports days. For those few hours it was just us, and she grew to become quite the champ. Pretty soon I wasn't letting her beat me, she had a real knack for it.

I still haven't been able to step foot in a bowling alley since.

Chapter Twelve:

Parkes watches as Atkins wolfs down the last of his fries, smothering them in sauce before popping them in his mouth. Clattering the cutlery onto his plate, he leans back and smacks his lips.

"I needed that," he says, trying and failing to hide a burp before patting his stomach.

"Sir, I don't think you're taking th-"

He waves away her protests as he stands, looking behind her. She turns to see a large bald man striding over, deep dark circles under his eyes. He shakes Atkins's hand as he introduces himself as Lenny. Parkes stands to give him the same greeting. He smirks slightly at Parkes, who pulls her coat tightly around her as he glances momentarily at her bosom. They move away to another table in the corner, leaving the girl working at the bar to clean up the mess. Parkes smiles at her as a thanks, but the girl is already blustering over the plates.

"So, what's all this then?" Lenny gives a sickly grin as Parkes joins them once again.

"You need an ale?" the girl shouts over to Lenny.

"Go 'ed," he smirks over at her, not even attempting to be subtle as he admires her bottom as she leans over to wipe the table they recently vacated.

As she trots off, his attention returns to the detectives. Atkins brings a photocopy of a picture from his jacket pocket. The picture shows Marie's kid in a school uniform, one she had kept in her purse since he left school the June before.

"That lad," Lenny pushes the paper back towards the detective and rolls his eyes after barely gazing down at it for more than a few seconds. "What's he done?"

"You know him?"

"No, but I had to deal with him last night."

"'Deal with him?'"

"Right mess, he was. He was doing my head in, so I gave him down the banks."

"You what?"

"Kicked him out, the wool."

"For what reason?"

"The lad was off his face. I knew it as soon as he came up to me. But he argued blind that he was sober. Then we got a tip off that he was sniffin' Charlie in the bogs. Was covered in sick, he was. Didn't like us kicking him out. Why you askin'?"

"He didn't come home last night. His mother hasn't heard from him since."

The expression on Lenny's face softens for a nanosecond, but once the drink is set on the table in front of him, he quickly collects himself.

"Well, I can't say I'm surprised. Considering how gone he was."

"You sure it was him?"

"Well, it was chocka. But I remember his face. Was the only one to give us grief all night. And I saw his ID. Lee something?"

"Wright."

"That's the one."

"Do you have any idea what direction he went in after you threw him out?"

Lenny shakes his head and lifts his drink to his lips.

"He walked towards Concert Square, but got lost in the crowd, like. Busy night last night, all the students back after the Easter holidays."

The detectives nod.

"Did he get into any fights?" Parkes asks.

"Just with me," he chuckles, before stating he was joking when he sees their sombre faces.

"He didn't rub anyone up the wrong way, bang into them on the dancefloor?"

"No, nout like that. Like I said, he was enjoying himself, just knew he was on something. Eyes were massive, like. Then, Tim gave us the tip off."

"Tim?"

"Little Indian fella works in the bogs. I actually don't know his real name. He saw him go into the cubicle and sniff a line. We know it's hard with all the students and that, but we don't like drugs."

He beams at Parkes, and she tries to smile back without the disgust showing in her expression. Something she fails. If Lenny could light a halo above his own head right now, Parkes is sure that he would. Thankfully, it seems that Atkins has got all he's came for.

"Thanks for your help, Lenny," he stands. "If you remember anything else, please don't hesitate to contact us."

The doorman merely nods his head before sipping his pint again as Atkins drops his card on the table. Atkins makes a show of waving goodbye to the girl behind the bar, eyeing up a few more selections of drinks in the process.

The detectives step outside and wander down towards the direction Lenny had said. The large square is still reasonably empty, despite several of the bars already being open. Music thumps from the huge clubs at one side, and the duo look down all the side streets that lead on to takeaways and different bars and clubs.

"He could've gone anywhere," Parkes sighs, slumping down onto one of the wooden tables and chairs in the square.

Almost instantly, a waitress in a black top skirts over, a huge grin on her face.

"Hi, girl. What ya havin'?"

"Oh, sorry. I'm not drinking."

The girl smiles before turning to Atkins.

"Get me a pint, please."

He sits adjacent to Parkes, who shakes her head.

"Helps me think. Get in the right mind frame, you know?"

He laughs, but she doesn't find it funny.

"Look, you can drive," he tosses the car keys onto the table, "it's only the one."

Truth be told, the beer in Bangers Bar had lifted Atkins's headache, making him think clearer. He checks his watch, it's only gone 1pm.

"I'd still say he's about here somewhere, don't you think?"

Parkes widens her eyes for a second to confirm she heard him, sucking her teeth in thought. Atkins thanks and pays the waitress when she brings him down the beer, and he's just raising it to his lips when Parkes hops up.

"Let's ask around. Someone is bound to know something."

And with that, she flounces over to The Lime Kiln, Atkins glancing at his pint wistfully before reluctantly joining her.

Chapter Thirteen:

The black and white chequered ground of Peter's Lane may as well be a zebra crossing the way she trots from shop to shop. From Hugo Boss to Michael Kors to The White Company to Karen Millen. Only the best for her.

I don't follow her into the shops, thinking it'd be far too suspicious the way she galivants back and forth between them. Returning for that fifth dress she tried on twice. Swearing she doesn't need it, but it'd be a waste when she has shoes that would match perfectly. I'm surprised there aren't burn marks on her credit card, the amount of times it's been swiped in the past hour.

Finally, when her and her friends have run out of arm and hand space for anymore bags, they're discarded under a table at Café Nero's outside sitting area. Pulling her purse out and winking at her two pals, raising her foot up in the air behind her with a kick, she scuffles off inside before returning moments later with three steaming hot cardboard cups. Fighting her legs between two of the bags, her head joins the gossiping girls, who shriek in hysterics and fan their faces as if laughter lines are dangerous.

I study her from behind a book display in the Waterstones. She seems happy. Her brown hair falling in waves with blonde tips. Her petite face caked in the latest eyeshadow and foundation. She's pretty, I'll give her that. But not as pretty as *she* would have been.

"Can I help you, sir?"

I jump with fright and almost drop the book I was pretending to examine. Turning to the attendant, I smile reassuringly.

"Fine, just browsing."

"We do have a seating area upstairs, if you'd like to finish..."

We both look down at the book in my hands as I twist it around to reveal its cover. Oh, God. *Fifty Shades*. I return my face to his with genuine shock.

"I... I..."

He raises an eyebrow and stifles a smirk.

"Wanted to see what all the fuss was about. Wife nearly chewed my hand off whenever I tried to take it off her."

The attendant seems disappointed as he nods and sulks away. I return the book to its display and glance back towards the girls, but their seats are vacated, their cups stranded on the stained silver table.

Chapter Fourteen:

"It's an absolute disgrace," Rebecca from Fairfield says, her rant almost drowned out by the persistent shoppers barging their way past, making her irritable but absolute gold for the audio recorder in Ashley's outstretched hand. "I shop in there all the time for all kinds of things for the kiddies. But now? They'll be lucky if they even get a glance out of me on my way past. Scallies, the lot of 'em, bringing that sort into our town."

This goes on for several more minutes than Ashley needs, but ever the professional, she nods politely in the right places in order to squeeze every bit of compliance from the petulant mum.

"Thank you, Rebecca. You've been a marvellous help," Ashley smiles, pocketing her trusty recorder once she runs out of steam.

"Will this mean I'll be on the news?" Rebecca's eyes light up.

"If we decide to use your clip, then yes. Six o'clock tonight."

"I'll be listening," Rebecca wags her finger with a grin before the ladies make a show of their goodbyes.

Ashley's fake smile drops as soon as her head is turned. She mustn't be ungrateful, however. As hard as it is to gauge public perception, Rebecca was the only one to give more than a few one-word answers. Voxpops can go from one extreme to another. Either you can't shut them up or no one will talk to you. Thankfully, Rebecca seems the type to be elated at the chance of being on the news. Ashley wouldn't be surprised if she's currently ringing all her friends and family to get them to tune in.

Turning again to Iskandar Bargains's shutters and sighing, Ashley brings out her phone to dial Matt's number for the third time since arrival. He answers on the fifth ring.

"Look, Ashley... I'm a bit tied up here at the minute."

"Just give me anything, please?"

"I'm no longer working on the Brown's case."

"What? That was quick. What's happened?"

"Well, to be honest, it's a done deal. There's no way Alvi's innocent."

"Well I could've told you that. But I mean why are you off the case?"

The tips of Ashley's fingers tickle like pins

and needles. She can almost smell the potential story.

"Off the record?"

"Of course," Ashley crosses her tingling fingers.

"We've had a missing person report."

Ashley's head drops a few centimetres in shock.

"What?"

"I know. We've got all hands on deck trying to work it out."

"Who?"

"I can't say."

"I could do a piece. I-"

"You'll do nothing until it's properly released to the press."

"Which will be?"

"I don't know. We're hoping it doesn't come to that. But you'll be first to know, alright?"

"Fine, thanks."

Ashley hangs up and grabs her bag from between her feet, trudging through the shopping precinct towards the food court. She mulls over her relationship with Matt whilst she bites into her salami sandwich. He had been a blind date two years ago that Jasmine had forced her to go on. Ashley had agreed on the off chance that she could shut her twin up, and even get a onetime fling out of her system. But upon hearing of Matt's profession, she had decided that he could be a lot more useful than a sweaty body for half an hour. Suffice to say, she has been stringing him along ever since. The odd *'x'* at the end of a text here and there, or a toss of her hair when they meet for an occasional *'no work talk allowed'* drink. Of course, like most adult conversations, the subject of work is always breached.

Her mobile phone on the table lights up to reveal a text message from none other than Matt himself.

'19y/o kid missing from last nite. Last seen at Bangers Bar. Press conference scheduled for 8am tomorrow if not found by then. Will call with more info soon xxx.'

Wrapping up the remainder of her sandwich and lobbing it in the bin, she canters out of the building. She hasn't whored herself out properly, proudly stating at a few work parties that she's only had to kiss him the once for some important information on a dodgy politician. But still, a source in the police always comes in handy, and as long as he keeps pondering after her, she hopes she can always get what she wants.

Chapter Fifteen:

Typing spitefully whilst glancing at the time again, Amanda sighs as she uploads another document from this morning's events. There's no way she's going to make it home on time to make Jade's dinner with all the paperwork she has left to do. Fat chance that Mike will make anything, so it looks like it'll be a KFC again, quashing Jade's diet she's been working on since Easter Sunday. It broke Amanda's heart seeing Jade drop off all her Easter eggs at her little cousin's house. She hopes she'll have the willpower to get a salad at least.

The front door swings open and she turns to smile at DI Atkins and DS Parkes as they scuttle in, soaked right through to their skin.

"Bit wet out there, sir?"

Atkins's demeanour doesn't diminish.

"What. A. Day," Parkes shakes the water from her hair over the welcome mat, brandishing the force's logo.

"No luck then?"

"We checked every pub, club and takeaway within spitting distance of the square," Atkins struggles to take off his sopping coat. "No one seems to have seen him. I'd say they drank at a party somewhere and went straight to the bar. Is Marie still here?"

"No, sir. I sent her home with a promise that we'll contact her as soon as we make any progress. We advised her to do the same."

"I hope so. Save us from running around half of the town in that rain only for the boy to be back in his own bed," Atkins huffs.

When the detectives finally make it up the stairs to their headquarters, they're just about to go into their respective offices when their names are called from the other side of the room. They turn to see DC Langridge waving over towards them.

"This better be good, Conor," Atkins growls as they join him at his desk by the window overlooking the Albert Dock.

"It is, sir. So, obviously we've taken Lee's phone number from Marie, and we've put a tracker on it."

DC Langridge spins around in his seat to give Atkins and Parkes a better view of his screen.

"However, the last signal was from Bangers Bar at 2:13am. That is... Until now."

Parkes's face lights up.

"About 20 minutes ago, it became active once again... Here."

His finger points at a map of the Edge Hill and Kensington area of the eastern city centre. And there, about a quarter of the way down Edinburgh Road is a green phone symbol with three lines protruding from the receiver.

"We've found him."

Chapter Sixteen:

The pounding on the door takes over from the pounding of the trance music. Niall breathes out in frustration, pulling his Chemistry book closer to him. Are people really still landing to party? It's been going on for Christ knows how long. How have they not burnt themselves out yet? Well, he knows the answer to that, with the sight of the dodgy looking bastard walking past his window last night when he was applying his hair gel. They've clearly been on more than a few tins. Niall had gone on a night out, got home and had a good few hours of sleep, had a shower and started revising all in the same time that they'd still been partying. The banging continues. Rolling his eyes, sliding off the bed and crossing the room to the window, he peers out as discreetly as he can towards the front door.

There stands a middle-aged couple with a uniformed officer behind them. Shit! They've really gone too far this time. The woman turns towards Niall's window and smiles. Thrusting his blinds back in place, Niall curses. She's seen him now. There's no way to ignore that. Sure enough, seconds later, there's a knock at the window.

"It's the peelers," Niall shouts through to the living room.

There's a scrabble of bodies and the music is shut off. Clearing his throat, Niall puts on his best fake smile as he swings the door open.

"Hello, there. My name is Detective Inspector Charles Atkins. This is Detective Sergeant Lauren Parkes," the man in the suit flashes his ID badge, the lady does the same. "I'm wondering if we can come in a moment?"

"Erm..." Niall smiles whilst pressing the door as close to his side as he can, imagining what disgraceful way the house is in. "Can't we talk out here?"

"We could..." the DI widens his eyes, "but I think it's better we talk inside... Don't you?"

Niall glances behind them at the nosy old git from across the street who has already shamelessly stepped out of his front door to get a better look at what's going on. No doubt it's probably him that rang them, out to survey his job well done.

"Er... Okay, okay. Come in, then."

Chapter Seventeen:

Parkes crumples her nose as she crosses the
threshold into what she hopes is a student house.
These houses in Kensington Fields are popular with
the students from John Moores and University of
Liverpool because of the close proximity to the
campuses, as well as the short walk into the city
centre. The Victorian style houses are ancient, so it
surprises her to see the old living room to her left
converted into a bedroom, which is rather neat
considering the rest of the house.

She trudges on through the hall, bypassing
a radiator hosting a clothes rail brandishing
different coloured sports jerseys. The stained carpet
looks like it's never been hoovered, and the walls
look damp. Following Atkins through to the living
room, she's greeted with five boys sitting down
with their heads bowed awkwardly. When she
passes them, they look up momentarily with shy
half smiles. Atkins and Parkes gather at the door
through to what they can presume to be the

kitchen. The floor is littered with crunched up beer cans, sodden takeaway boxes and stained plates. She struggles to hold in a retch at the sight of a cup at her feet with mould growing in the contents.

"Big night, lads?" Atkins's voice booms through the silence.

The boys glance at each other expectantly, nervously chuckling. The biggest of the lot, seemingly taking up most of the sofa, coughs to draw their attention to him. He wears a Republic of Ireland football top, white trunks and his feet are bare.

"Sorry about all the noise, officers."

Parkes wonders if all the lads that live here are Irish.

"It's just that it's Tiernan's birthday," he nods his head towards the boy slumped on the wooden picnic chair, whose eyes expand in dismay. "We might've taken it a bit too far. What time is it, anyways?"

"It's shortly before five."

The boy whistles.

"Jay-sus. Well we've nearly been on the lash for 24 hours. We apologise, it won't happen again."

He beams at the officers, displaying a perfect set of white teeth. A charmer, Parkes thinks.

"Well, that's all well and good," Atkins coughs, "but that's not why we're here."

The boys glance around distractedly, before resting their eyes on the lad who let the officers in.

"What?" he shrugs.

"Niall, what are ye playin' at?" another boy chips in.

"I thought it was because of a noise complaint?" Niall holds his hands up.

A few of the boys groan and mumble things under their breath, one even throws a half-drank tin towards Niall, the contents spilling all over his tracksuit bottoms.

"Now, lads, come on. Listen to me," Atkins's voice grows grave.

It works, all attention returns to him.

"I'm here because I'm looking for Lee Wright."

They had already scoped out the room, and with no sign of Lee they guessed that he may be in a bedroom upstairs. However, all of the lads share confused looks.

"Don't know him," another boy with a thick Dublin accent calls out.

Bringing out the photocopy, crinkled and sodden now that it's been in and out of Atkins's wet pocket all day, he passes it around. Each face is met with the same look of unrecognition.

"We've traced his phone to this house," Parkes blurts out, nervous now that all the boys are staring at her.

"Oh... That could be me," the heavy boy levers himself off the sofa. "It might be the phone that's upstairs in my room. Let me go get it."

71

The two officers, both willing to escape the disgusting living area, follow the lad uninvitedly up the two flights of stairs.

"I found it lying outside Bangers Bar last night. I'd... Erm... Helped a girl who had dropped her bag. I saw a phone lying on the ground and thought it was hers, but she was halfway down the street by the time I picked it up. Well, one thing led to another and she ended up back here with me."

He finds it hard to suppress a smile, something that turns Parkes's stomach. They make it to the two rooms on the third floor.

"Sorry about the mess," the boy says, before pushing through to the room on the right.

Atkins looks back at Parkes and raises his eyebrows in amusement before joining him. Snatching the iPhone from the charger on the single bedside table, the boy turns and hands the smashed phone to Atkins.

"Before the girl left this morning we had to decide which phone was hers. She had this one in her bag. Must've picked it up thinking it was hers. So, to decide, we had to charge both of them. She recognised the background on hers and took it home with her. I was gonna bring it back to the bar, I promise."

Atkins nods his head in fake approval, before pressing the home button on the phone. Sure enough, the wallpaper on the phone shows four lads in a nightclub, a professional club photograph. And there in the middle, underneath the white numbers displaying the time, sits Lee Wright smiling up at them.

Chapter Eighteen:

Rounding the corner from her apartment block, Leah's first sight is the impressive grand display of Liverpool Lime Street Station's side entrance, before marching up Skelhorne Street. Despite the constant flow of black cabs barrelling towards her, Leah still half-jogs up the steep incline, wrapping her jacket around her tighter. With the blinking streetlamps, this can be a daunting place at this time of night.

As she reaches the T junction where the road meets with Copperas Hill, she pulls the collar of her jacket higher over her face. Inching her gaze towards the corner of the building, she's relieved to see that the apartment seven floors up is still in darkness. Her flat mates haven't made it home from their night out just yet. A new spring in her step, she continues the few moments journey until she's met with the zigzag road layout that makes her thankful she didn't bring her car to university with her.

Waiting for the green man, she brings out her phone to let him know that she's around the corner. He uncharacteristically texts back immediately, giving her the code to the front door. Heart in her throat, she passes the instantly recognisable St Andrew's Gardens, infamous within the student scene for resembling a Spanish bullring. Rounding Greek Street, her shaking hands pin in the code she had been repeating over and over in her head since he sent the message. The light blinks and she shoves the heavy door open. When it closes behind her, she's greeted with silence. The automatic light takes a few seconds to click on and she sends another text.

'*Inside.*'

It's read within seconds, the three dots confirming his typing in reply.

'*Well hurry up then,*' with the winky eyed emoji.

Trying desperately to steady her breathing, she climbs the stairs two at a time, holding onto the handrail for support. She'd been waiting for this moment since October. Whenever she felt ready to move on from the heartbreak of moving away from Sam, and her new bunch of flatmates convincing her to make a Tinder profile. She activated it, but another drama that ensues living in a flat with six other girls in their late teens engulfed the next topic of conversation.

Leah had forgotten all about the app until days later. She logged in and got to work. Meticulously clicking onto guy's profiles, reading their interests, scanning through their pictures and trying to figure out how far away those number of kilometres were. She had no idea how Hayley could scan through man after man that fast, her thumb a blur as she made a nanosecond decision on whether she was staring into the face, or chest, of Mr Perfect or not.

Several unsuccessful matches later, Stuart presented himself. 20-years-old, dirty blonde hair, and a wide grin that got Leah tingling. Seeing that they shared similar interests in music and movies was a bonus, so her first successful swipe right was confirmed. But no sooner had the next random suitor popped up, she had a notification. They had matched. She squealed girlishly before composing herself, clicking on his profile and thinking about what to say as a greeting. The small vibration on her phone confirmed she need not have worried, he had already popped up.

'Alright, gorgeous?'

What followed was weeks and months of flirty messages and dirty talk. Even the odd nude here and there. She guessed uni really does change people. If Sam knew she was at such things, he would be completely appalled. But maybe that's why she liked it? But Stuart was flaky. He cancelled plans at the last minute, and there were times when she'd be at the bar waiting for their date and he just wouldn't show or reply. He'd send a half-hearted apology days later, stating something came up. She'd simmer for a few days, daring herself to delete him, but he always found a way of crawling back into her good books.

The other girls were more disappointed than she was. Bargaining with her to search for others. Trying to push her into groups of lads on the dancefloor when they were out. Consoling her when Stuart cancelled again and again, telling her to never arrange anything with him in the future. That's why she had pulled a sickie tonight. They were all heading into town for drinks and a boogie. She was up for it until he messaged her.

'Wuu2 tonight?'

He had done it countless amount of times before, only to leave her in bed on her own fuming at him, and herself. But something about tonight felt right. She just knew that they were going to finally meet and shake off this stupid dance they had found themselves in. She feigned sick and sat on the sofa in her pyjamas, urging them to go, checking her phone every 30 seconds to see if he'd left the gym. Finally, they bade her farewell, kissing her on the head and giving her a group hug, before tripping down the corridor. As soon as she heard the bang of the fire door on their departure she was on her feet, sprinting to her room to find something sexy to slip into. A few sprays of perfume and her good makeup, the one her mother told her not to ruin on drunken nights out. When he finally replied to say he was home and showered, she was already in the courtyard, sitting on a bench in angst of being seen by someone she knew and having to explain herself.

Now, here she is. Outside door number 14, too afraid to knock. Counting down from three, she finally finds the strength... Nothing. She starts to panic. Has she gotten the wrong room? No, it's definitely number 14. She had memorised it. Is this some sort of joke? She looks up and down the corridor and coughs slightly, before backing off and making a start down towards the stairs. But a shadow appears in the small gap between the door and the tiled floor. She holds her breath. After a few seconds of sounds of scrambling keys, the door is open and there he is. His smile instantly makes her toes curl, and he's standing in nothing but a pair of red boxers. She can't resist but look him up and down, trying and failing to hide a smile.

"Well, are you going to come in?"

She nods dramatically, giggling again as she crosses the threshold and Stuart shuts the door with a sharp click.

Chapter Nineteen:

Despite the light drizzle flicking off the huge window overlooking the Wood Street entrance leading to Concert Square, the crowds of party animals have already started to gather. Either venturing further into the square or going into O'Neill's for one last pint, Atkins watches them all from the snugness of his huge comfy chair in the bar inside the Hanover House. Girls who clearly aren't locals struggle over the cobbles in their heels. Rivalling club promoters with their logo hoodies thrust over their ears from the cold, allies for a moment to greet each other and huddle against the wind.

Atkins drains the residue at the bottom of his pint and hiccups as he stands, striding over not so steadily towards the long bar. With a hand on the bar-top for good measure, he thrusts the other into his back pocket, scavenging for loose change for another round. Tony nods his head in Atkins's direction and makes straight for the taps. That's when Atkins notices he's being watched. A lady in a black and red bulging corset is smiling at him from the other side of the bar. Smirking back and skidding around the corner to stand beside her, Atkins gives his toothiest grin.

"What's a beautiful girl like you doing standing at the bar on your own?"

"Waiting for a lovely lad like you to buy her a drink?"

Atkins laughs at the corniness of it all and turns to Tony, who was momentarily confused by Atkins's change in position.

"Whatever this lady's having."

"Gin and tonic, please."

When the drinks have arrived, he asks her to join him and they flounce back over to the seats overlooking the street.

"Wouldn't fancy standing out there too long like some of those young ones," she says, sitting down and crossing her legs.

"Especially in that get-up," Atkins chuckles, nodding and staring too long at her exposed breasts.

"I know," the woman smirks, "I'm a bit overdressed. But I've just been to the theatre next door."

"The Epstein?"

Atkins spent many a night in the audience watching Olivia dance in pantomime's in the Epstein throughout her primary school days.

"Yeah, myself and my friend Lily were watching a mutual friend of ours, Ivy, there. She stars in some lovely plays."

"And where are they now?"

"Well, Lily's had to go home to relieve the babysitter, and Ivy's been held up with the press. I'm supposed to be meeting her in here actually..."

She spins the top half of her body to gaze around the bar, Atkins letting himself steal another glimpse at her bulging top.

"And your name?"

She smiles and turns back towards him.

"Rosie."

"Are all your friends named after plants and flowers?"

Rosie bursts into a fit of giggles.

"No, actually. It happened completely by chance. And you? What's your name?"

"Poppy."

Another explosion of laughter from Rosie, with many heads surrounding the two turning, but Atkins doesn't care.

"No, I'm Charles, actually."

"Nice to meet you, Charles," she extends her hand dramatically.

Chapter Twenty:

As the shudders of Stuart's body slowly subside and his panting returns to normal breathing, Leah expects the stillness and stiffness of his body to relax. Instead, he slides off her and instantly stands, searching the room for his boxers. He finds them where he left them, discarded at the door. Leah perches herself on one arm and smiles at him, but he won't meet her eye. He rolls the condom off, his back to her, and wraps it in tissues before lobbing it in his waste bin. Straight over to his bedside table, he brings out a white pair of trainer socks and pulls them on. Coughing nervously, Leah decides to dress as well, her clothes all in a pile from where he had instantly stripped her. By the time she's buttoning up her blouse, he's pulled on a university branded hoody and has started to strip his bed.

"Ummm..." Leah starts, expecting him to turn around.

He just stiffens more, as if that were possible.

"I had fun?"

He nods. She turns her head and wipes a tear away, pretending to inspect the contents on his desk.

"Oh, you've been to Egypt?" she picks up a framed photo of himself and who she can only guess are his family with a vista of the pyramids behind them.

"Yeah."

"Great, wasn't it?"

"Suppose so."

"Our guide was a right knob. Made us sanitise our hands after touching anything."

Another nod as he shoves the sheets deep into his wicker clothes basket, before turning and finally facing his body in her direction. His eyes, however, looking at the window, his bottom teeth biting his top lip sullenly.

"So..." she elongates the word, "it's getting late. I best get off."

Almost instantly he claps his hands and heads for the bedroom door, his white socks sliding over the wooden floor easily. When he gets to the front door he spins around and smiles slightly at her, his eyes resting about a half inch above her head.

"I'll text you," she smiles leaning in for a kiss.

He panics and inches his cheek towards her lips, banging off them aggressively. She narrowly misses biting her tongue and makes a fake sound of content before crossing the threshold, a slither of a goodbye escaping her trembling lips. He mumbles something in reply as he shuts the door.

Hammering down the stairs before they become blurred by the tears, Leah pushes the door open just as the first wail escapes. Leaning against the wall of the flats, she tries to calm herself. How could she do this to herself? Be used like this? What did she think was going to happen? After everything that he'd done to her, he was suddenly going to be Prince Charming and be the perfect gentleman? Let her take him home to meet her parents? She had been so stupid, and now she won't be able to talk to the girls about it because she had betrayed their trust. And she hasn't even spoken to Jenna and the girls back home since Christmas. She can't just text them out of the blue with this.

Pulling herself together as a taxi honks past, she lifts up the hood of her coat and steps forward, making her way home back the same way she came. On the other side of the street she can see a fogged up green Clio, and narrowing her eyes to see better, she feels like the shadow in the driver seat is watching her. She stops, suddenly afraid for her safety. She thinks about returning to the flats, she still remembers the code to the door, but could she make it back on time? Should she keep walking? Phone the police? Is she being overdramatic? Overcautious? Her anxiety flaring because of the situation she's found herself in? All the uni reps that came to her school deemed Liverpool a safe city... But with that boy on social media going missing... She brings out her phone and presses it to her ear, pretending she was stopping to answer a call. She doesn't take her eyes off the car until, moments later, it reverses around the corner and speeds off into the direction of town.

Chapter Twenty-One:

The pair talk for over an hour. Rosie refuses to be bought drinks after they begin to get to know one another and agrees to take it in turns. They talk about everything as the street outside starts gathering with more and more young people, the next more drunk than the last. Atkins staring into her deep green eyes. Sometime before midnight, when Atkins is on his way back from the bathroom, he sees Rosie collecting her belongings, swinging a massive white puffy coat over her shoulders.

"Are you leaving?"

"Yes, sorry. I forgot that I have a big day at work tomorrow."

"Me too. Please, stay for one more?"

"I can't, I'm sorry. I need to be home soon."

"What are ya, Cinderella?"

That laugh again. The one Atkins longs for.

"I'm really sorry, but I've had a great night."

She leans towards the door and Atkins grabs her hand.

"Can I have your number?"

"I've left my phone at home and I don't know my number, I'm afraid. It's a new phone."

"Then can I at least give you mine?"

She smiles sheepishly as he writes on the back of a beer mat.

"Will I see you again?"

Atkins feels like he's in some stupid rom-com Kaitlyn would've forced him to watch.

"It depends," Rosie tucks the beer mat into her coat. "I *might* be here on Friday night?"

"You '*might?*'"

"Maybe," she chuckles with a wink.

When Atkins leans in she shrieks with delight before running out of the door.

"But what about your friend?"

Atkins spreads his arms wide, but it's too late. Rosie has already jostled herself into a black cab, waving out at him as he resumes his seat beside the big window.

Chapter Twenty-Two:

"A 19-year-old male has been missing from the early hours of Wednesday morning," Atkins squeezes his coffee mug a little too tightly, showing his nerves. "Lee Wright was last seen outside Bangers Bar on Slater Street after 2am, after attending a party with friends just off Smithdown Road. At the moment, we aren't treating his disappearance as suspicious. However, we would like to hear from anyone who was in contact with Lee on the night, or since. Every lead is useful."

He coughs and brings his hands away to pull at his shirt collar, unaware that some contents had started to spill onto his fingers, and leaves smudges of coffee on his crisp white shirt.

"This is an appeal to Lee himself, if he's watching," Parkes leans so far forward into the mic that the unpleasant squeak of feedback echoes through the room, leaving the journos digging a finger into their ear. "Please contact either your mother or the station to let us know that you're safe. You aren't in any trouble. She is very worried about you. You don't have to tell us where you are or why you didn't come home on Tuesday night, but just let us know that you're alright."

The manager of the Adelphi Hotel looks between both officers before standing and coughing.

"We will now open the floor for any questions."

Ashley Bell's hand is straight up.

"Why aren't you treating his disappearance as suspicious?"

"We have no reason to," Atkins narrows his eyes at the reporter, fully aware of her persistent need to make every operation like an episode of Brookside.

"So, what do you suggest happened to him?" Ashley crosses her arms, Dictaphone still resting on her lap.

"Well, we all have a best-case scenario that he simply lost track of time. Has gone from party to party and is hopefully on his way home now," Atkins smiles through gritted teeth.

"So, kidnapping is out of the question? Runaway? Suicide? Murder?"

"There has been nothing to suggest the sort, Miss Bell. We'd like to keep a level of optimism in this investigation-"

"So, what you're saying is that you aren't pursuing every avenue?"

Atkins breathes out heavily, the sound just about reaching his mic, luckily Parkes sits forward to take over before he loses his temper.

"What the inspector is trying to say is that there is no evidence of any crimes of the sort being committed here. Of course, God forbid, something has happened the boy, then we will leave no stone unturned. We have notified uniforms on the ground and the docks have been searched but to no avail. This is merely a conference to see if we can get in touch with him or anyone who knows where he may be. You, as the press, have a level of duty to spread the word. Get people talking. You'd be surprised of the results."

"Where's Mrs Wright?" another reporter with a neatly combed moustache who she recognises from the Echo chips in.

"She's still at home in case he returns. She wanted to come today, but we suggested it was best that she stayed at home."

"And Lee's father?" Ashley raises her eyebrows.

"With his wife," Parkes smiles, not disclosing that his wife and Marie Wright are different people.

The station's PR officer then makes a stand and collects the journalist's attention as the two detectives are led out of the hall by the manager, who gushes about how thankful he is that they decided to choose the Adelphi for their conference. Ashley's are the only eyes that follow them until the door to the function room is snapped shut behind them.

Chapter Twenty-Three:

Stepping outside of his university building, Simon gazes up at the beauty of the Metropolitan Cathedral. He used to go here all the time with his grandad, who played the organ sometimes when his friend Abe was sick. But whether he was watching his grandfather fill the huge room with beautiful notes, or squashed between both him and Nan, Simon spent every Sunday until he fell sick there.

"Hello!"

Blinking away the memories, Simon turns to see Taylor and a few boys from his classes standing chuckling at him.

"Sorry. Was miles away. Hi, mate."

"What's gotten into you? I were callin' you for ages."

"Nothing, nothing. Tired just."

Taylor observes him for a while longer before nodding.

"Sound, pal. You poppin' down to Hardman Street for ciggies?"

"Uh, yeah. I suppose."

Turning away from the cathedral and walking quickly to keep up with Taylor and his friends, Simon walks a few paces behind them as they snigger about their tutor, who expects some big assignment before next Thursday. Taking a shortcut down Maryland Street, Simon looks longingly at the library and stops to consider his options. Taylor and co trod on, laughing and playfully pushing each other.

"I'm just gonna head in here, T. Got an essay that needs doing."

Taylor doesn't hear him, so he calls again. Giving up, he storms up the steps and around the corner to the entrance. Slamming his student card on the system, the plastic barriers skirt sideways to let him past. Climbing the stairs and finding a quiet corner with a free computer, he throws his bag down just as his ringtone blurts out. An agitated Asian student growls at him before turning back to his mathematic problem. Pressing the silencer before he brings it out of his pocket, Simon gets angrier when he sees it's Taylor.

Throwing it onto his desk, he looks onto the street outside to see Taylor and his friends standing just a few yards from where he left them. His friends are rolling their eyes and jerking their heads in the direction of the shops. Taylor finally nods and replaces the phone in his pocket, the light of a missed call displaying on Simon's screen as he tries hard to distinguish his angry thoughts and tears.

Chapter Twenty-Four:

The waving of Ryan's hands tell Todd that it's now recording, as if the small beep and red LED light from the camera hadn't already tipped him off. The room is instantly filled with people rambling recited scripts, and Todd is just about to burst into his own segment from *When Harry Met Sally* when he spots two people staring in the door of the studio. Knocking quietly, they step in and apologise to Amber, her face growing solemn as they break their news.

"Er... Alright, guys. Very good. I just need you all to take a quick break now. There are detectives here that want to have a chat with you all."

A few confused faces step back from the equipment and trudge forward towards the intruders. Todd lingers at the back, a sickness in his stomach as he pleads for the couple to not say what he knows they're going to say.

"For those of you who may already know, we're looking for a missing person," Parkes announces when they introduce themselves. "He's actually a classmate of yours, Lee Wright."

Gasps and widening eyes from the crowd.

"Has anyone heard from him since Tuesday night?"

The class look from left to right to see if anyone responds.

"Okay, so the next thing we'd like to ask you is if anyone was with him on Tuesday night, when we think he went missing. We understand a lot of you go out then because you're off on Wednesdays. Yes?"

A few sombre nods in the crowd.

"Okay, so if anyone who went out with Lee on Tuesday night could step forward please."

Two people step forward reluctantly, glaring at others who they know were also out.

"Okay, thanks guys. Now can we just stress that you aren't in any trouble here. We aren't going to judge you for where you were or what you were doing. We're just here to find Lee. Anyone else care to bring themselves forward?"

Four more people step forward into the no-man's land before Todd gulps and takes the leap forward.

"Great, guys. Thank you for your honesty. So, if there's no one else?"

The accused look behind to their peers, trying to see if anyone is lying. Anna shakes her head and beams at the detective.

"Okay, can we just steal you guys for a little while? I promise it won't be long. Looks like you're very busy," she nods her head towards the cameras and smiles again at Amber.

They then lead the friends out of the room, Todd being the last to leave and hear Amber join people who have lost their pair with another.

Chapter Twenty-Five:

He walks with such... What do the kids call it these days? Swagger? He looks like a bleedin' idiot. His grey beanie hat barely visible behind those neon headphones. And the combat shorts? It's freezing, what is he thinking? I curse at the red light as he rounds the corner of the Empire Theatre, but it's a relatively straight road down to St George's Hall. It's there where I could lose him.

Finally, the lights turn green and I swirl around to only be met with a row of more traffic. Why did I think it was a good idea to drive around at lunch time? I should've parked up somewhere and pursued on foot. His headphones are a nice touch now, actually, as I can make him out in the crowd. He stands outside the converted Spoons, before ringing someone on his mobile. I'm level with him now, so staring isn't a good option. Rolling down my window slightly, I catch the tail-end of his conversation.

"Oh, man. Really? I'm a dumb shit, be there now. I'm at the wrong one," he laughs.

Hanging up, he waves at me as I let him cross the road, one hand covering my face so he can't see me, pretending I'm blinded by the sun, which is behind dark clouds. Dodging a bus, he starts his way down towards St John's Gardens and I know instantly where he's going. An easy mistake, I think, pulling into the car park at the precinct and ignoring the honks of a black cab that just misses the back of my latest stolen vehicle.

Chapter Twenty-Six:

"What the *fuck* are we supposed to say?" Ryan reveals his palms as he thrusts his arms in front of him.

"Just tell them the truth, Ryan," Anna shakes her head at him. "If we lie we could incriminate ourselves, or worse, fuck up this investigation."

"And maybe Lee won't be found," Louis adds.

"Incriminate ourselves? Do you want to go to jail for taking Charlie?"

"You can't go to jail for taking drugs, ya scab."

"Oh, really?" Ryan says sarcastically.

"Yeah, 'course not," Jake rolls his eyes.

"You can go for possession or selling," Louis continues, "but if we say we just took it there's nothing they can do. Besides, they've already said that we aren't going to get in trouble."

"Oh, they say that all the time. In reality, our parents and 50 other police officers are hiding behind a one-way mirror listening."

"Oh, grow up, Ryan," Todd shakes his head. "You've been watching too many bizzie shows. We're doing what's best for our mate, and that's the end of the story. Alright?"

Ryan sighs heavily before jolting his head towards the window, his arms folded in a huff.

Moments later, Laura comes out of the office and heads straight for the hall, not looking anyone else in the eyes. Parkes steps out and smiles at Todd.

"Would you like to come in next, hon?"

Chapter Twenty-Seven:

Falling into a booth adjacent to his in the Spoons opposite the Queen's Square Travel Centre, I bring my phone from my pocket and download a basketball game to pretend to play to avoid any stares from people wondering why I'm here alone. He's seated behind me with two other lads, one with what I guess is a Manc accent. Seems he hasn't saw one of them, Gav they call him, since leaving school the June before.

They don't talk about anything significant, just girls, footie and university. He seems to be keeping his nose clean, which is more than I can say about my little friend the other night. I saw his face splashed across the telly when I was standing ordering my pint. Cops asking people to come forward if they know of his whereabouts. Seems my trail was quite clean... For now. I don't want to jinx anything, but I heard on the radio in the car earlier that his disappearance isn't being treated as suspicious. But the longer they go without hearing anything from him... They might stick their noses where I don't want them.

The crack over his head that the rod made still echoes through my mind and I hide a smirk with the froth from my pint. There wasn't much of a struggle after that. Quick and easy, he was knocked out. Don't know whether he was dead, but the journey up to the farm with the car was undisturbed. Afterwards, I took the car off the track and torched it in a field. I haven't heard anything about it on the news or social media yet, so either it still hasn't been found or the disappearance of the boy has been taking precedence.

"Hi, lad. What about that boy Lee who's gone missing?" Gav says, I'm guessing from glancing at the TV screen in the corner.

"I know, mate," the Manc chips in. "Did yous lads know him?"

"He looks familiar, like," *he* says, "but I don't think so. He's a wool."

"A wool?" the Manc asks.

"Someone not from the city," Gav explains. "From St Helens was he? Or is he, I should say?"

"No, mate. Widnes."

"Arr, lad," Gav laughs, "proper woolyback that, like. Why's it all over the news here for?"

"Went to school here, the news bloke was saying. And was out in town night he went missin'."

"Rough that. Do they think he's topped himself?"

"No idea, mate. Just saw it on the Echo's Twitter page when I was on my way in. Anyway, you gone see your mam while ya 'ere?"

Conversation returns to normal, and I realise that I'd been holding my breath, my heart beating violently in my chest. Breathing out as discreetly as I can, I drain my pint and stand and exit as inconspicuously as I can, not wanting him to recognise me from the car before.

Chapter Twenty-Eight:

Todd's foot taps impatiently below the desk. His eyes circle the room, determined to look anywhere but at DS Parkes's face.

"So, Todd. If we could start from the beginning, please?"

Todd nods, his gaze on the poster advertising the bake sale next week.

"We met at Ryan's house in Smithdown."

"Where exactly, please?"

"Cumberland Avenue. Lives there with his brother."

Parkes gives a reassuring nod for him to continue.

"Started having a few ales there. Taxis were booked for 11 o'clock. I think Lee got into one of the first ones. Ryan, Anna and I were the last to leave. By the time I saw him in Bangers Bar... He was bladdered. Proper gone, like."

"Were you taking any drugs?"

Todd holds his breath.

"I'm not going to arrest you. You aren't even in any trouble, I promise you. I just need to know what state of mind Lee was in."

Todd sighs his exhale.

"He was snortin' blow."

"Cocaine?"

Todd nods again.

"And I think he was taking a few pills."

"And where did he get them?"

"Left the party to get some."

"Do you know who he bought them from?"

"No. And I'd say we'd get into proper trouble if we told ya."

"I understand. Does Lee know them?"

"I'm not sure. I'm not trying to cover my own back here, but I tried it once and it weren't for me. Gave me a headache."

"We aren't putting you in a corner here, Todd. You aren't on trial. We're just trying to cover this investigation from all angles."

Atkins, who has been relatively silent up until now, last night's drink still sweating from him, observes Todd until his own phone blares from his pocket. Parkes shoots him a look before he apologises and leaves the room.

"Did anything happen? Was there a... Scuffle?"

"No, nout like that. Lee just ran out to the dealer's car and grabbed some and brought 'em back. Him and some of the lads went upstairs to take 'em."

"No money was owed? Anything like that?"

"No, not at all. They were going on about how cheap they were."

"So... The person in the car... The dealer? There isn't a chance that he could have something to do with this?"

Todd shrugs as Atkins comes back into the room, re-joining Parkes at the other side of the table.

"Fine. Did he seem strange in the club? You know... Apart from..."

"Being rottin'?"

Parkes smiles and nods.

"Not really. He was happy, like. Just havin' a boogie and a laugh and that. Then the doormen came and shuffled him off. I tried to grab a few of the lads, but they were too smacked out too. By the time I got outside, he was long gone."

"And you haven't seen or heard from him since?"

"No. I texted him asking if he got home alright yesterday morning. But heard nothing back. He hasn't even read the messages on the group chat either. When I saw you guys coming in earlier, that's when I started to panic. He'd always be online, phone stuck to his hand, like."

The two detectives nod and tell him he's excused. Atkins stands with him and closes the door instead of calling their next interviewee.

"A lady has called the station. Was working in the Subway on Bold Street the other night. And guess who came in and made a right ruckus?"

Chapter Twenty-Nine:

By the time Simon's getting the 82 bus back from town, he has had three more missed calls from Taylor. Feeling the phone vibrate vigorously in his pocket just makes him more and more angry.

They've been best friends for coming up to five years now. Ever since Miss Applegate's History class. She was a new teacher straight out of her PGCE and so made the class sit in alphabetical order in a desperate attempt to remember their names. She forgot them anyway, of course.

Taylor was cool and collected, swinging on his chair and biting his pen. Simon was nervous and fidgety, fresh out of hospital and forced to repeat a year to catch up on the work he'd missed. They didn't speak for the whole first lesson, Taylor constantly getting told off for turning around to flirt with Hannah behind him. He'd always had a thing for her. The next lesson, Taylor had nearly slipped whilst swinging on his chair, recovering quickly but biting down on his pen too hard, the ink squirting all over his face, shirt and desk. Simon tried desperately to hide his smirk, but pretty soon they were both in hysterics, hiding their giggles behind their textbooks.

Ever since then, the two have been inseparable... Or *had* been inseparable. Simon didn't really get on with Taylor's other school friends, he thought they were scallies, but just went along with it and pretended to like them. They didn't repay the favour, but until their final year, Simon also had his friends from the upper class, or his original class, had it not been for his hospital stint. So, when final year came, he spent more and more time with Taylor, and became more and more frustrated at his friendship circle.

Of course, when you've just turned 18, you start to head out with your friends to parties and clubs. Taylor's friends would get into fights and Taylor would sometimes join them, but Simon just went home. He thought once they were at university that things would change. After all, all of Taylor's friends were going down south to study. But he'd fallen in with a new group, and he didn't seem to mind making the same mistakes again, despite Simon reiterating them to him any chance he could get.

Hopping off the bus at South Parkway, Simon's eyes bulge as he sees Taylor standing waiting for him at the doors. Damn that new Snapchat update that lets you track your friends.

"What's up with ya?"

"Nout."

"C'mon, Simon. Tell me," Taylor swings his head in Simon's direction as they start the short walk home.

"Just had an assignment to do."

"And you wouldn't answer your phone?"

"Was busy."

"Why'd you bugger off without tellin' us?"

"I did. You weren't listening."

"I didn't hear ya. Can't blame me for that, mate."

Simon quickens his pace.

"Mate, come on. Don't get all mardy."

"I'm not."

"What's really botherin' ya? Is it 'cause I was with the boys?"

Simon doesn't say anything.

"It is, ain't it? Oh, come on, Si. I promise you, they aren't that bad. Not one bit."

"I get a really bad vibe from them, T."

"You're just scared of the past repeating itself. Look, we're heading out tonight. Why don't you come out with us too? Heading into town again just for a while. You up for it?"

They've reached Taylor's gate, but Simon just waltzes on past. Taylor hurries to catch up, before grabbing his arm.

"Please, mate? You'll see they're not so bad."

Simon sighs. It would be good to spend some time with him again, it has been a while.

"Fine."

"Great, pal. I'll text you the details. See you later."

Simon watches him trot into his house, trying desperately not to look at the ass of his tight jeans, before scurrying up the road towards his own home.

Chapter Thirty:

The Nando's in Liverpool One is always a good shout, hungover or not. Leah sits with the girls, catching up with their drunken antics and getting stuck into her chicken wings and Peri-Peri chips when her phone vibrates loudly on the table. Only Hayley notices, glancing down to see the notification with Stuart's name.

"No, Leah! Do *not* reply."

Leah's heart drops, she was hoping to delete the message with everyone being none the wiser. But now everyone has stopped their mini conversations and have turned to Hayley.

"What's wrong, Hayls?"

"It's Stuart. He's just after texting Leah."

A few gasps circle the table and Leah nervously shoves the phone into her jacket pocket.

"It's no big deal, he still does sometimes."

"And do you reply?"

She shrugs.

"You *do*, you slut!"

113

Leah rolls her eyes at Hayley, dipping her chips into the medium hot sauce.

"You seriously don't think he's any good for you, right?" Melissa leans forward, patting Leah's arm.

Ever the mum of the group.

"Nothing's going to come of it."

"I hope not. He's not worth your effort anyway, judging by the size."

Leah gawps at Hayley.

"What do you mean by that?"

"Well, let's just say I saw a picture over your shoulder one time. It wasn't my fault," a few of the girls shriek with laughter, one even throwing her napkin in Hayley's direction. "You weren't very discreet about it. If you're going to continue this stupid celibate scheme, at least wait for a man who's packing."

The girls continue to laugh, Leah even joining in for a bit.

"It must've just been the angle. It's... alright," she smirks.

A few stop giggling and stare at her.

"How would you know that?" Morgan asks.

Shit, Leah thinks.

"Er..." she starts squirming. "Different photos. Different angles."

"Your face is beetroot," Hayley leans forward, her mouth agape. "You slept with him, didn't you?"

114

Leah blows a raspberry and squints her eyes, but the girls explode.

"Oh. My. God."

"What the fuck?"

"When the hell did this happen?"

"You really are a slut."

When they've calmed down, Leah shakes her head.

"Just... Last night."

"Last night!" Roxy screams, a little too loudly, the table beside glaring over.

"Sshhh, yeah. He texted when I was in bed. After you guys went out. I thought... What the hell? Might as well get the first rebound out of the way, y'know?"

Leah reaches for the straw in her coke, before twirling it around nervously. She doesn't like lying to them.

"And how was it?"

"Hayley!"

"What?" Hayley jabs her hand in Roxy's direction as Leah chuckles, "we were all thinking it."

"It was... Good."

"Really?" Hayley's eyes expand. "Well, I guess this is only your second time."

"It isn't my second time," Leah blurts.

"Okay, okay. Well second time with someone else. Sam might've been terrible."

"Fuck you!"

The table start to giggle again, their chicken abandoned.

"But... After we finished..."

Leah wasn't going to tell them this part, but the cat's already out of the bag.

"He... He just didn't talk to me. Wouldn't even look at me. I left shortly after and just felt like a complete idiot."

Leah's surprised to feel tears start to prick her eyes. The girls moan in unison, Melissa even skirting over to drape an arm around her.

"And what did he say? Just now?" Hayley narrows her eyes.

Leah reads the message out loud.

"*'Out having a few bevvies with mates, think they're catching their train soon from Lime Street. You in?'*"

"Dickhead!"

"Asshole!"

"Needle Dick!"

The latter came from Hayley, and the girls erupt into laughter again.

"Well," Hayley picks up her Fanta, "now that we've got the first one night stand out of the way, let's get you back on the market. I know this guy, awful tattoos, but you might like him..."

Tucking her phone back into her jacket, Leah smiles through the tears as the girls start tearing Stuart to pieces. Exactly what she needed after a sleepless night of self-loathing.

Chapter Thirty-One:

Atkins can't help but detest the awful multi-coloured lanterns strung around the TV frame on the wall as he enters the living room of Sophie Chen's flat. She's draped in a dressing gown, the hairnet from last night's night shift still hanging from her ponytail.

"I'm sorry it took me so long to contact you. I was working until 4am last night, and then I went straight to bed. Only seeing the news on social media when I woke up," Sophie nods to the detectives as they settle onto her uncomfortable dining chairs, made that even more awkward with the too-high cushions thrown on top of them.

"Don't apologise, I'm sure it's a stressful enough job dealing with a load of drunk people every night," Parkes smiles at the lady.

"I'm sure you understand to some degree," Sophie nods back.

"So, I'm guessing you have some information about Lee Wright?" Atkins leans his head to the side.

117

"Oh, yes, yes," Sophie nods again.

Is it a nervous tick?

"He paid our Subway a visit. After half two on Tuesday night. Or Wednesday morning, if you prefer. I know as I'd just come back from my break."

"So that's after he left Bangers Bar," Parkes sighs.

They had questioned the guy who worked in that Subway towards the latter part of yesterday afternoon, but he had said he wasn't working and asked the manager, who shrugged his uninterest, before returning his attention to the agitated customer complaining about the lack of hearty Italian bread.

"I'm guessing," Sophie nods, taking the sergeant's statement as a question. "They definitely wouldn't have let him back in. He was off his face. Slurring his words. And his eyes? They were huge. He was definitely on something other than a few pints," she nods again.

"We've established that," Atkins shakes his head, "can you tell us what happened?"

"Well, there was a big queue, naturally at that time of night. But he barges to the front and asks for his sandwich. I tell him that he'll have to wait in line like everyone else. My colleague, he's on his break, so it's just me. He starts being very aggressive. This boy, he confronts him. They start arguing, and then another one gets involved. Pretty soon there's a whole brawl. I'm screaming at them

118

all to get out, get out. They do, and last time I saw Lee he was on the ground with the two boys beating him."

"I guess you didn't catch their names?"

"No, but one of the lads came back in and ordered some food."

"And the other?"

"They'd both disappeared by the time I had a look out of the window again. Like I said, very busy. I work there at night and study during the day. I need to pay bills. No time for staring out at drunk people fighting. Would never get anything done," she laughs and nods her head three times.

"Okay, looks like these guys are our new persons of interest. I'm guessing the fast food place has CCTV?"

Chapter Thirty-Two:

The creak of the stairs makes Jennifer jump in a panic. Pulling herself off her bed as quietly as she can, she throws the new shoes she was admiring into a desk drawer. Flopping herself back down and shoving a pencil in her mouth for good measure, she opens her textbook at a random page. Just in time too, as she hears the door snap open. Glancing up, she sees her mum slouched against her door frame.

"Alright, Jen. What you up to?" she hiccups.

"Just doing a bit of studying," Jennifer smiles.

"Anything interesting?" her words are slurred.

"Nope, just the Cold War," she looks down and curses herself.

The page is open at an artist's representation of The Battle of Hastings. Hopefully, in her mother's drunken state, she won't notice. But it looks like she isn't going away. It's not even dinner time yet. How long has she been drinking?

Her mum waltzes in, grabbing a picture from the top of Jennifer's bookshelf, the one of the two of them at the beach, shortly before her father left.

"I love this picture," her eyes are brimming with tears.

Using the opportunity to strategically close her book, Jennifer crosses the room to embrace her mother.

"What's wrong, Mum?"

"Oh, nothing... You know? I just miss him."

"I do too. Has something happened with Geoff?"

Since the divorce, Jennifer's mum has had a string of relationships with anyone who would have her. But she meets the majority of them at the PTA fundraisers and meetings. Divorced single dads or widowers who are looking for nothing but a bit of fun. Jennifer's convinced Geoff is even stealing from them.

Jennifer has tried to show her mother that she's going the wrong way about finding love, but she'll never listen. She's showed up drunk to Amy's school now four or five times and Jennifer's confident that she won't be allowed on the board much longer. Maybe that will be the kick in the teeth she needs to get her life together? Or spiral it into a deeper hole.

"He never came over last night when he said he would. I haven't heard from him all day, and this afternoon I realised that my jewellery box is

121

missing. I searched everywhere for it, but it's gone. All my good jewellery's in there, you know that. Especially the rings your father bought me, those are worth thousands."

Jennifer whistles in shock, then gives her mum another pat on the back.

"You could try the police?"

"There's no use. I went to the PTA meeting earlier and asked the principal, Luke didn't come to school today. Luke and Geoff are probably long gone by now," she pulls away and sniffs, gazing out of the window onto the street, as though visualising them driving far, far away from here.

Jennifer gets a stab of guilt as she takes a quick glance at the drawer concealing her new Louis Vuitton shoes, but she quickly shakes it from her brain. After all, it isn't her or her mother's money she's spending. There's no harm in that, is there?

Chapter Thirty-Three:

Once Simon has completed the inevitable and predictable display name, about and age on his profile, he narrows his eyes at the remainder of the requirements. *'Body type?' 'Position?' 'My Tribes?'* What the hell is a *'tribe?'* He flicks through the options, getting just as confused with every reveal. *'Leather.' 'Otter.' 'Poz.'* He shakes his head and clicks *'twink,'* the only one he's heard of. Even though he'd say he's a little thicker than your average twink.

That complete, he swerves past the questions about his sexual health, not wanting to embarrass himself by writing that he's a big fat virgin. Photo time. Oh, no. He turns the flash off and takes a quick shot of his white sheets. Nothing too incriminating with that picture. Satisfied, he clicks upload.

He raises his eyebrows at the endless possibilities. Picture after picture of guys in his area. Although petrified at the thought of even meeting up with any of them, he feels safe behind the anonymity of his screen. There are quite a few blank profiles and strategically taken pictures that reassures him that a few others are in the same boat as him. A ping indicates that he has a message straight away.

'dysondave59: alright lad?'

Simon turns his nose up at his picture. He must be at least 60. Another few tones flood through. Jesus, imagine the response he'd get if he'd even uploaded a photo? But then again, if it was a selfie, he could be getting fewer. Or none. Maybe these lads think there's a good bit of meat on the other side? No one catches his eye as he scrolls through the messages.

'27: hi.'
'c2c?: you pic?'
'marty m: hung?'

He stares baffled at the last message. Whatever happened to subtlety? Disgusted, and uninterested in the picture message that *'bigbarry'* sent, he clicks sign out, before turning and burying his face in the pillow. What is he going to do? Nan is persistent in asking him if he has a girlfriend yet.

"What's keeping ya? Good looking boy like you," she will chuckle, before offering him a hard boiled sweet to suck on.

He hasn't even came out to Taylor yet. He wants to... But the childhood fantasy that Taylor will actually feel the same is too overpowering that he knows he'd get disappointed with any other response, even if it was wholehearted acceptance. And imagine what Taylor's other friends would think? They'd hate him and exclude him even more than they already do. He'd never get a chance to hang out with Taylor.

Pulling his hands out of his trousers, he decides he *will* go out with them tonight. He had only told Taylor that he would just to shut him up, but now he's changed his mind. He will act loud and laddish and scallyish and then maybe, just maybe, he can fit in.

Chapter Thirty-Four:

The student house on Jubilee Drive that Adam Davies lives in with his girlfriend, Rachael Hall, is a lot tidier than the one inhabited by the Irish lads, despite being only a stone throw away. Parkes vocally admires the plush pillows masking the ripped leather settee as she nestles down with a cup of proffered tea.

Rachael had contacted the station after the CCTV footage from outside Bold Street's Subway was shared on social media earlier this evening. The *'leak'* was a motive by the police to get the faces of the two lads who got into the scrap with Lee out there. Rachael was one of the first on the phone.

' To eliminate us from your enquiries,' she had assured them.

As Parkes sits looking at her blustering over the watermark on the coaster on the coffee table, she can't help but question if this is a double bluff.

"Adam should be home soon," she smiles sweetly before Parkes has a chance to ask, "big project at uni is due tomorrow, so he's been at the library all day. Wouldn't have had a chance to check his Facebook, but I gave him a ring and told him you were coming. That should light the fire under his ass."

Parkes fakes a chuckle.

"So... You saw Lee on Tuesday night?"

"Yeah, we were in the queue in the Subway on Bold Street when he charged in. Started screaming at the girl behind the counter. Me and Adam both work in retail at the weekends to help pay for this place," she gestures around her, "so we know how annoying customers can be. Adam started to get really angry with him, but I made sure to calm him down. Well... I tried. Obviously, it went on too long, and he just snapped. The boy was being really rude and aggressive, and then he started mocking the girl's accent. That's when Adam stepped in. He gets really irate about that because... Well..."

She points at her face to indicate her swarthy complexion.

"Right..." Parkes nods, encouraging her to continue.

Sophie Chen hadn't mentioned this.

"Adam told him to back off, and tried to get him to leave, but he was having none of it. Started kicking off at Adam, and then another lad got involved. One thing led to another, and then that boy Lee made a swing for them. The Subway girl kicked us out after that, and I was screaming at Adam to stop once Lee was on the ground."

Parkes had seen the footage, and although highly pixilated and with no sound, it was obvious that Rachael had made no indication to stop her boyfriend from attacking Lee. She had just played with a stray bit of hair as she watched, not unlike how she looks now perched on the dining room chair.

"Lee was still hurling abuse, though. Calling them scallies and that. When he finally shut his mouth, we went to the chippie and then got a taxi home. I still have the booking from the app on my phone if you need proof."

She plucks the charging lead out of her phone in the corner of the room and types hurriedly before brandishing the screen at Parkes, who makes a note of the times and driver registration.

"That's the last time we saw him, I promise. He was out of his face, so I can't imagine he would've got home easily... But this is taking the hand a bit..."

Rachael blinks her sympathetic eyes slowly, whether genuine or not, Parkes can't decide.

"Thank you, Rachael. I obviously want to stay and speak to Adam too, if you can hold off on your dinner for a little while yet?"

Rachael nods feverishly, before busying herself with clattering around the kitchen, shouting through that she's sure there's a packet of Kit Kats in there somewhere.

Chapter Thirty-Five:

Atkins stubs out his cigarette as he brings out his phone once more. He knows he should be with Parkes speaking with the girlfriend and guy who actively kicked the shit out of Lee the other night, but the long day of interviews in the stifling hot college classroom had made his headache worsen. Saying he was going to try contacting the father again, with several unsuccessful attempts already recorded, he had needed a pint.

Now, here he sits outside McCooley's, the Irish bar on Concert Square, four drinks in. The fog in his head has just started to clear as he sips the head of the beer and strains his eyes against the light from the sun. Not a cloud in the sky. Should he call it a day? It's lovely sitting here. It won't be getting dark for another hour or two, that's plenty of time for a few more. And after all, the Superintendent is constantly on his back about cuts and overtime.

Once he saw the boy, Adam or whatever his name was, walking away from Lee in the footage, he just knew it was a dead end. Not bothered to chase it, he had sent Parkes, who was still full of life and concern over the case. It's getting a little tedious, if truth be told. He just wishes the boy would come out of hiding, shout surprise and be done with it.

If Atkins was a betting man, one of the few life ruining demons that he hasn't succumbed to yet, he would give Lee another 12 hours before he pops up. Been staying with a mate. Wanting attention. After all, his dad clearly doesn't give a shit about him. He needs to get it from somewhere. Maybe hoping it will help bring unity between the families? Build bridges and all that? He's so deep in his own thoughts it takes him a second to realise the ringing on the end of the phone has stopped.

"Er... Hello?"

"Hello."

"Hello?"

"Hello, who's this?"

"Er... sorry."

He's disorientated, the drink taking its toll. He had completely forgotten that he was trying Lee's father's number again. He uses his thumb and his fingers of his free hand to crush his eyes together to refocus his attention.

"Yes, hello, Mr Fowlie. My name is Detective Inspector Charles Atkins from Liverpool Police Department. I'm calling in regards to your son, Lee

Wright."

"Who?"

The line is dodgy enough, but it sounds like Fowlie is somewhere with a lot of background noise.

"Detective Inspec-"

"No, I heard that part, mate. Who are you ringing about?"

"Lee Wright."

There's silence from Fowlie over the line, the distant sound of club music the only thing Atkins can hear.

"Yes, I'm still here," Fowlie sighs as Atkins brings the phone away from his ear to check the signal before addressing him once more.

"Have you been in recent contact with your ex-wife, Marie?"

The snort is just about audible over Fowlie's loud surroundings.

"You must be joking."

"Mr Fowlie, have you any idea that your son is missing?"

Fowlie is silent once more. Atkins squeezes the phone to his head and pushes a finger into his other ear to hear better as it sounds like the phone is being travelled about. The next time Fowlie speaks, the background noise has disappeared.

"Lee is missing?"

"Yes, Mr Fowlie. Now, I know this must be upsetting for you, bu-"

"I have nothing to do with it."

Atkins narrows his eyes.

"I haven't said you had, Mr F-"

"Look, I haven't seen the boy in over a decade. I have had nothing to do with him since he was eight or nine. Marie made sure of that. I mean, I sent the odd Christmas and Birthday card because my wife guilt tripped me into it... And that stopped after he turned 16. I promised myself it would be the last. Since then, there has been no contact whatsoever. I don't even have the boy's number, for Christ's sake. So, I'm sorry to hear about his disappearance... But I'm afraid I'll be of no use. I'm sorry, but I'm very busy at the moment. I'm working. Is there anything else?"

Atkins stares at the collection of students sharing a fruity flavoured shisha. This does not sound like a man who has found out his son is missing. He's so dismissive and uninterested. Surely no one can be that cold?

"Er... Okay. Do you not want to hear of any progress that's been-"

"No, frankly, I don't. Whatever's going on with the Wrights, I want nothing to do with it. I escaped that life a long time ago. Now, if you don't mind, I'm getting back to work."

"Okay, thank you Mr Fowlie. Please be sure to keep your phone on in case w-"

The beeping indicates that Fowlie has already hung up. Atkins curses and shoves his phone back in his pocket, a niggling feeling at the back of his head. Not because of Fowlie's reaction, but because of something else. Something obvious. He lifts his drink to his lips just as his ringtone blares out.

"Parkes?"

"Sir."

"Any luck?"

"No, sir. The girl has a receipt on her phone of the taxi home. And her story matches the boy's. Of course, we'll be contacting the taxi driver for confirmation, but they both said they have nothing to do with it."

Atkins nods before he realises that Parkes can't see him.

"Very well, Parkes. I've just come off the phone to Lee's old man. He wants nothing to do with the investigation and is very defensive in claiming his innocence in it all."

"Strange."

"Yes, I want us to look a bit further into their relationship. I feel like there's something he's hiding."

"Yes, sir. I'll get on that now."

"No, Parkes. Go home and spend time with that beautiful baby of yours. We can resume tomorrow."

The reluctance is apparent in Parkes's voice as she bids him farewell. As Atkins drops his phone on the wooden table in front of him, that's when he realises what was annoying him. When he'd rang Fowlie, the ring back tone wasn't the strange one you're met with when ringing someone on holidays. It was the same as your standard UK call. Fowlie isn't in Spain. He's back home.

Chapter Thirty-Six:

The look of annoyance and disgust can't be hidden from Taylor's mates' faces as Simon trots up Church Street, a few steps behind Taylor.

"Alright, T?"

One of the bigger ones, Dempster Simon's sure he's called, gives Taylor a cringey high five.

"What all we been at then?" Taylor sits on the bench beside them whilst Simon hovers awkwardly to the side.

"Just got a Maccies, mate. Not been home yet," Dempster kicks his bag further beneath the bench for effect.

"Your mam and dad still giving you abuse?" Taylor lights a smoke.

"Yeah, man. Flat out givin' off ever since they found that bag of brown in my trousers. Didn't believe me when I told 'em it was yours."

Simon stares appalled as Taylor mocks annoyance before kicking Dempster in the shins.

"Ar la, don't be at that, mate."

Simon, remembering his mission of trying to be one of the lads, coughs aggressively. Even managing a crude spit at their feet, which makes the woman walking too closely beside him to gawk at him with revulsion. She tuts and struts off, head in the air.

"Clueless ol' bat," Simon shakes his head, chewing imaginary gum.

Dempster half-nods towards him in affirmation, lips pursed.

"So, where we going?" Dylan stands up, his arms behind his head in a stretch.

"Dunno, la. Where's good on a Thursday?" Dempster says through biting his dirty nails.

"I heard Baa Bar has got a promo night on," Simon nods, shuffling his hands in his pockets, remembering what he had read on Facebook on the bus on the way in.

"Aw, I've not been to Baa Bar in years, like," Freddie smirks. "Not since that night Cat shadowed me everywhere. That's when they had them same-sex cubicles down the back, mind? Even followed me in there."

The lads laugh and Simon forces himself to snort along.

"You know what?" Taylor winks towards Simon, "Baa Bar sounds like a good shout. Then we can go 'round the corner to Woody's when we're pissed for a bit of karaoke. Mines is Robbie Williams Angels."

Chapter Thirty-Seven:

"Another?"

Atkins nods his confirmation to the pretty waitress as she shuffles back over to the bar, taking his two empty glasses with him. Flicking through his wallet, he sees he has no more money. Shaking his head at the printed page above the bar with Jokerman font stating cash only, he groans upon her return that he'll have to go to a bank machine. She smiles back and tells him not to worry, still escorting the cold pint back regardless. He meanders down cobbled Wood Street, excusing himself as he fails to supress a large burp, upsetting a few ladies walking towards him.

Closing one eye to see better, he gazes across the road to the bar inside the Hanover House. He wonders if Rosie will be there. Still annoyed she hasn't been in contact, he makes a mental note to be there as early as he can tomorrow night in the hope that she does show up. Trotting up towards the wonky crossroads where Hanover Street branches left to Church Street and right towards Bold Street, he stops and observes the hustle and bustle of a Thursday night on the street where Lee Wright was last seen. So many shops and takeaways. So little information. Someone is bound to have seen what's happened. Making his theory about his disappearance being deliberate all the more credible.

Crossing the road at the lights, he joins the long queue for the ATMs. Realising he needs to pee, he jiggles his legs apprehensively. The cold wind doesn't help. He jabs his head around the side of the queue, sighing deeply when he sees two blokes having a full-scale conversation and not realising there's a free machine. Rolling his eyes, he looks further down Church Street and sees that the queue for the ATMs outside Santander half a dozen metres away is much shorter. He skirts over, set on joining the back of the queue when he misjudges his speed and loses his balance. He falls backwards before catching himself with his other foot, waving his hands around to steady himself.

"Watch yourself, mate."

He'd accidently brushed across someone's chest in his fit to stay on his feet. He turns around to apologise to whoever it is to see five young lads chuckling at him. The taller of which, he is shocked to see, is the second guy from the CCTV tape. Atkins can't speak, he just goggles at him.

"Piss head," the boy in the black hoody he had almost taken down laughs again, before the boys resume their journey, leaving Atkins to stare after them.

Seconds later, he finally pulls himself together. Following them at a safe pace, he wonders what he can do. He's far too drunk to be able to ask to speak with him. He'd be a laughing stock. Maybe he should call in another officer, but hounding him on the street in front of his friends wouldn't look good for the force. Especially with no good evidence or reason to do so.

Atkins winks and waves apologetically at the waitress outside McCooley's as they turn left at The Lime Kiln. Before they reach the crossroads where Bangers Bar rests, they flash their IDs at the bouncer and enter a bar thumping with music and lights. Atkins gazes up at the neon sign above. He's never been here before. And with good reason. Everyone inside look to be in their late teens. The doorman raises his eyebrows at him as he stands outside. He must think he's lost. Although the huge windows look onto the scene perfectly, the boys are quickly swallowed up by the crowd. Cursing, Atkins smiles briefly at the doorman, who steps aside with a roll of his eyes.

Once inside, Atkins scans the room. A huge staircase juts out from the far right wall, with a long bar dominating the left. In the middle are several tables with stools scattered around them filled with young people splashing multicoloured liquid from shot glasses as they *'cheers'* one another. Craning over heads, he quickly finds the boys gathered at a table towards the back. But with no vacant surrounding tables, and not to mention the loud rap music, Atkins doesn't know how he'll be able to get close enough to them without arousing suspicion, never mind actually hear anything. Instead, he totters over to the furthest side of the bar, anxious that they might spot him.

After a few moments, a girl wearing the logo shirt tied in a bow to show a toned stomach with a glittery navel skirts over.

"What ya havin?" she shouts.

Atkins's stare is broken as he looks at the girl. Shit.

"Erm..."

He looks down at the bar top with one eye closed to see better. It's overtaken with a long laminated menu of drinks.

"Give me a..."

He blows a raspberry. They all seem disgusting.

"Exotic Bingo."

It had the fewest ingredients. The girl raises her eyebrows before nodding and turning around to prepare his drink. He looks back up to see the fivesome heading towards him.

"Fuck!" he mutters, resting his elbows on the sticky worktop and shielding the majority of his face with his hands.

When he looks up again, he almost misses the back of the shorter guy heading up the stairs.

"Two quid, hon," she sloshes the shot glass down in front of him.

Shit, he forgot he has no money.

"Five quid minimum for card payments, babes," the girl strains a smile as he brings out his card.

Atkins exhales exhaustedly.

"Get me another two, then."

"We've no more pineapple juice, I'm afraid," the girl shrugs after a lazy look over her shoulder.

"Then get me two more..." his eyes fall on the first one he sees, "Brain Damages."

The girl purses her lips at his bluntness. He taps his foot impatiently as he watches her talk with her colleague, who doesn't try and be discreet when he glances over towards him. Atkins widens his eyes at him in an attempt to telepathically tell them he's in a hurry. When she finally brings over the shots, which look even worse than the first with things actually floating around in the liquid, he batters the card off the machine.

"No contactless, doll."

It's like she's intentionally trying to annoy him. He jabs his pin in hurriedly as she takes her sweet ass time handing him the card, and his receipt, back. He gives her a passive aggressive thanks, before pinning the three shots, stifling a gag upon the last, and thunders up the stairs. He's

142

met with a body of people obstructed by smoke and strobe lights so fast it looks like everyone is dancing in slow motion. Every time he tries to find his bearings, he's once again shoved to one side. Not even getting a chance to apologise to whoever it is he's tripped over, he is engrossed in the waves of bodies and featureless faces and stands on several other people's toes again.

Ten minutes later, a deflated Atkins steps out of the bar and starts down towards the square once more. There was no way of finding him in there. Especially trying to be subtle. Something very hard in his drunken state. Admitting defeat, knowing he's in no shape to organise anything further, especially with his upset stomach swirling around God knows what, he flags down a black cab and rests his throbbing head in his hands. He has to get his life together... And soon.

Chapter Thirty-Eight:

They have no idea I'm watching them as they neck shot after shot. As they wolf whistle at girls. As they hit the bottom of their bottles off the necks of their friends' bottles so the beer comes shooting out like champagne. The latter somehow meriting a cackle of laughter. Idiots.

It's mad actually being inside. Not watching from afar for once. Well... Far enough away that I can voyeur unnoticed. Watching in plain sight. I don't know what he's doing with these bunch of dimwits. Out of everyone, I thought he was the good one. The one who would give me the least trouble. The one who seemed clued in. But looking at him now with these bunch of scumbags... It's hard to distinguish between them.

I bite the inside of my mouth to control my anger. How dare he? Resort to this appalling behaviour? Whilst in his everyday life he puts on a show of *'the good kid.'* A shitty actor. And an even shittier closet case. Does he really think no one knows? Pretending to look at passing girls' asses to fit in. Clinging to his friend and gazing into his face every time something happens. Yearning for his attention and approval. He makes me sick.

A girl stumbles towards me, her eyes closed, breaking my contact with them. I step aside to let her past, but she still manages to bang into me. I unjustly apologise through gritted teeth as she smiles up at me. Wrapping her arms around my neck, she leans in for a kiss. Stepping out of her embrace, I jog away and down the stairs. What is wrong with people? Why would you ever want to get yourself into states like these? And on a Thursday fucking night? I know if she were here, she wouldn't be like these animals. She'd be civilised.

I calm myself down in the corner of the room, only to see a few boisterous boys laughing and pointing at me. I faintly hear the word *'paedo'* carried towards me through the music and the shouts. Shaking my head, I step out into the crisp night. The streets are a lot more crowded than they were a few hours ago, when I followed them here. I pull my coat around me and bury my face into it to keep warm. Thankfully, the doormen are busy jostling with people in the queue and checking their IDs to notice me as I rest against the wall beside the sign for Fleet Street... Waiting.

Bradd Chambers

Chapter Thirty-Nine:

"For fuck sake!"

Finally managing to twist the correct key in the lock, Atkins falls unceremoniously through onto the wooden floor of his hall. Swimming through the letters, leaflets, bills and takeaway menus he hasn't bothered picking up in weeks, he kicks the front door closed with a loud bang, which echoes through the lonely house.

He gazes about him as his head lulls around until it connects with the wall behind. There are muddy footprints on the stairs that have caked themselves into the woodwork. A spider nestles contentedly inside its web perched precariously between two of the spindles on his bannister. The giant black and white picture of himself, Kaitlyn and their girls overlooks the entire hallway.

He looks into his eyes. Into Kaitlyn's smile. They were happy then, weren't they? The girls certainly look happy. Olivia's tiny white teeth missing at the front as she beams at the camera. Michelle grabbing her sister's hand with a gummy grin, her hair in the signature front bobble all little girls seem to rock before it grows out properly. All of them sporting the signature white t-shirt, blue denim jeans and bare feet that most professional photographers are entranced with. Despite the fact that Kaitlyn had actually went out of her way to go to Next for new outfits for the girls.

He groans as he struggles to his knees, crawling through into the living room. Nestling into the surprisingly comfortable groove he somehow managed to make for himself last night with the couch cushions and old throws, he finally lays his head down. Remembering his alarm for tomorrow, he needs to be in the office for 8am sharp, he's running the place for Christ's sakes. Struggling to bring his phone out of his back pocket, he clicks the alarm clock icon, before continuing into contacts, lingering over Kaitlyn's name. It takes all of his energy not to click *'call.'* After all, he is trying to prove to her that he is a responsible father. Calling her in the wee hours of the morning pissed out of his brains hasn't worked well so far. And currently having to have supervised visits to see his own flesh and blood? It is ridiculous.

Deciding tonight isn't the night, he drops his phone carelessly onto the cushion, where it slides off and makes a large thud as it misses the teddy bear coloured rug. Sighing loudly, he stops fighting with his batting eyes and gives way to sleep. Knowing tomorrow will be another day where he has to prove to everyone that he's okay. Especially to himself.

Chapter Forty:

"Oh, I wanna dance with somebody."

The lads laugh ludicrously as Simon struts in front of them, clapping his hands in the air and hopping along the cobbles, still singing Whitney Houston.

"Y'know, the boy's alright," Dempster nods to Taylor, who beams with delight.

Simon marches over to a parked car and pulls at the handle, seemingly surprised that it is unlocked, as he falls backwards onto the ground to another whoop of laughter from the boys.

"Here, lads. Look!"

Kyle stretches the door out further and points inside. The other four gather around.

"What's that?"

"New sneaks."

"Aw, they're right my size too."

"Rob 'em."

"We can't do that."

"Why can't we not?"

"Yeah, stupid div left his brand new trainees in an unlocked car in the middle of town. He's asking for it."

And with that, Kyle lifts the trainers out of the box, slams the door and hides a shoe under each armpit.

"Ar, la. You're crazy man," Dempster laughs, bringing out his phone and uploading a video of Kyle awkwardly sauntering down Seel Street to his Snapchat.

When they're safely inside thriving Nabzy's, the busy chicken place on Hardman Street, Simon gets a quiet moment with Taylor.

"Taylor, this ain't right," Simon says, trying to keep his voice down, but too drunk to realise how loud he's being. "They're nickin' stuff."

"I know. It's only a laugh. Calm down, man."

"Nah, T. This isn't right. I don't want any part of this. I had a good night, but I'm going home now. Fuck this."

"Don't," Taylor grabs Simon's arm as he goes to break away. "Dempster was just saying the boys were enjoying your company tonight, la."

Simon narrows his eyes at him. He's never said *'la'* to him.

"What you mean?" his curiosity getting the better of him.

"They said you're alright. A laugh and that," Taylor looks ahead at the three of them chuckling away with the server as they collect their meals.

Pursing his lips, Simon nods as he holds the door open for all five of them.

"Will we see if the Hope and Anchor is still open?" Taylor suggests.

The three ahead nod and skirt left down Baltimore Street and towards the bar facing the library. The street is eerie at night, with the odd jutting out purple bin and empty keg from the surrounding bar making it easy to bash into. Much to the delight of the other boys. There's a few more cars too. Emboldened by the drink, Simon jogs forward and decides to make a show again. They think he's *'alright.'* Could it just be the drunk goggles, or could they finally be accepting him? The Polo closest to them has locked doors, but he fetches a leather jacket from the half-open window, which he throws towards Taylor to the laughs of the boys. Reaching the Honda, he pulls at the driver's door just to be met with a piercing alarm. He jams both of his hands to his ears and turns to see them all making a run for it.

"C'mon, Si!" Taylor sprints back towards the direction they came from.

Head down, intent on joining their retreat, he misjudges how much of the car bonnet he has bypassed and flies straight into it. Falling to the ground, both his hands go towards his throbbing knee as he curses in agony. He leans back his head and tries desperately to straighten his leg, a searing pain flying through his body every time he does.

Biting his bottom lip until he breaks skin, he tries another few times. Giving up, keeping the knee elevated and his foot on the ground, he leans his head back. It's awfully light. And he feels like he's going to be sick.

He opens his eyes to look up at the night sky. But what is that amber flashing light? The sound of the car alarm suddenly floods back into his consciousness. Shit. He needs to get out of here. He goes to roll over to try and see if he can crawl away. But before he can, out of nowhere, a big black boot connects with his head, which is ricocheted backwards off the ground and suddenly his knee isn't the problem anymore. He can definitely taste blood now.

"What the-"

But his protests are lost. Because when he opens his eyes again, he sees a looming foot coming crashing down onto his face.

Chapter Forty-One:

Everyone's excited whispers come to a stop as DI Atkins slinks into the incident room, DS Parkes at his heels.

"Kieran Fowlie, father of missing Lee Wright, is *not* in Spain, as his ex-wife, Marie, insists."

A few looks sideways and gaping open mouths is exactly what Atkins was expecting.

"DC Langridge, our IT expert," Atkins jabs his pointed pen towards the front row, where Langridge looks around seemingly embarrassed before nodding his head, "kindly chased this up for me in the early hours of this morning. Now, when I gave the man a ring yesterday, it was a UK calling tone which greeted me. That had tipped me off. Langridge has since traced the call, which was taken from a Chinese restaurant in St Helens. The mobile has been very much active around these parts for a number of months, to say the least. Therefore, I want all eyes on him. Check his bank statements, his call logs, his friends and relationships. His wife, Becky, is seemingly still in Spain. We need someone to make contact with her. See if they're broken up. And if so... Why? DC Gregory, can I delegate this to you?"

DC Gregory nods in confirmation, writing the lady's name on his notepad.

"In the meantime, I'm going to be paying him a visit. We've managed to track down his address to a flat just south of Huyton. While I'm doing that, DS Parkes here will be speaking to Lee's mother, Marie, again."

Parkes raises her eyebrows in astonishment. She was under the impression that she was going to be joining him.

"Everyone else, I need this man's life picked apart. Anything odd or peculiar, send it my way. Class dismissed."

As there's the signature scraping of chairs and rustling of papers, everyone vacates the room except for Parkes and Atkins.

"Questions, Parkes?" Atkins barks.

"Yes, sir. Why are we speaking to Marie again?"

"'cause the man's been home. Maybe he's made contact? Maybe he's kidnapped the boy? Maybe the boy's went running to him? Either way, she might know something. Keep at her. I've got to go, traffic out there will be a nightmare at this time."

Atkins coughs and excuses himself as he slides out of the room, leaving Parkes with nothing but confusion and the stale smell of drink in his wake.

Chapter Forty-Two:

Either the scruffy handwritten surname haphazardly shoved into the frame beside the doorbell for 5C hasn't been changed, or Fowlie has moved address without their knowledge. Atkins ponders whether to click and disturb whoever this *'Parnell'* character is before an elderly woman, clutching a white Scottish terrier in one arm and half a dozen ASDA bags for life in another, struggles out of the door. Atkins reaches and holds it open as she thanks him.

"Lovely young man," she gives him a gummy grin as she reaches down to attach a lead to the dog's collar.

"You're very welcome, miss."

He couldn't remember the last time someone had referred to him as *'a young man.'* Almost as soon as the woman groans upright again, the dog makes a go for the main road, making the woman grapple with the lead handle, her arthritic hands shaking as she lets out a soft *'ooft.'*

"Persistent little character, is she?" Atkins chuckles.

"He," she corrects him, smiling down at him as he circles her feet. "Yes, loves getting out to the shops. Especially on a day like this, where we can take a stroll through the park."

Atkins lolls his head to the cloudless sky. It looks like it's going to be another good day.

"You the new boy?"

Atkins returns his eyes to the stooped over woman.

"Sorry?"

"5C?" she brandishes her curled in claws at the list of names beside the doorbells.

"Oh, no. I'm not. That's why I'm here actually. I'm looking for him."

The woman nods and resumes talking like a baby to her dog, reassuring him they'll be on their way soon as he wags his tail and slobbers over her brown shoes, groaning impatiently.

"I'm guessing you don't know a lot about him?"

She shrugs.

"Don't like talking about folks I don't know."

"I see he hasn't even changed his name on the list here... Suspicious, don't you think?"

She shrugs again, avoiding his eye.

"I'm sure he's busy. We've just heard him come and go."

"We?"

Atkins hopes she doesn't mean her and the dog.

"The other residents. Keeps himself to himself. Works long hours it seems. Heard him troop past my door before seven this morning. Heavy feet, y'know? Haven't heard him come back, so you've no use checking here."

Atkins nods as his phone blares out, deeming the woman's use fulfilled as she excuses herself and finally gives in to her dog's demands.

"Langridge?"

"Sir. It seems that that Chinese restaurant in St Helens is Fowlie's place of work. I've found online payslips dating back as far as five months. If he's not at home, maybe that's the next place to look?"

Atkins thanks him, before hanging up and shuffling over to his car. As he enters the restaurant's postcode into the SATNAV, he pulls left only to halt at a zebra crossing, waving pleasantly at the old lady and her dog crossing in front of him, trying to ignore the suspicious look on her face. Hopefully she's as in the dark as she says she is and doesn't tip Fowlie off to their enquiries.

Chapter Forty-Three:

The monotonous tone of Steven's voice doesn't penetrate the barrier of Taylor's brain on any given day, but especially not today. And not because of the hangover. With his file open in front of him, he holds today's handout upright, masking his phone in his other hand.

It's been over eight hours since Simon was last online. He hasn't read any of Taylor's messages or answered any of his calls. Taylor had half a mind to knock on his door before uni this morning, but didn't want to worry his nan. Thoughts of sleeping off a hangover or forgetting to set his alarm dispersed immediately. This is Simon he's talking about. He would never do such a thing. It would be completely out of character, and besides, Taylor knows that he should be in his 9am lecture down the hall from him now. They would've sat beside each other on the bus in, something they've done every week since September.

When Taylor had regrouped with Dempster and co at the bottom of Hardman Street last night, stitches in their sides and their food abandoned, Simon was nowhere to be seen. After calling him on his mobile several times, Taylor was encouraged to continue back down towards Seel Street to another bar. He kicks himself for it now. He should've went back up to find his best mate. But influenced by the drink and the Charlie, Taylor had decided that Simon must have went through with his threats to go home. After sending him a text asking him to let him know when he got home safe, Taylor had joined the lads for another few drinks, before getting a taxi home himself.

Even Simon's snap maps hasn't been updated, meaning he hasn't been on the app, Taylor thinks frustratedly, as he zooms out of his avatar joining a few others resting in the current uni building on the corner of Hope Street and Mount Pleasant. But even zooming into Simon's house, his avatar has completely vanished.

"Taylor?"

He looks up to see a sea of eyes staring up at him from his seat in the lecture theatre, including Steven's, who is gazing at him with a bored expression, his hands resting on the table at the front of the room.

"Er... Yeah?"

"I asked you a question."

He shuffles in his seat.

"Sorry, I wasn't listening."

"A given," Steven rolls his eyes as a few chuckle, before nodding to John a few rows in front.

"Africa?"

"Yes, well done, John."

Taylor's phone bursts to life, vibrating rigorously on the table. Grabbing it and pressing it into his legs to stifle the echo, Taylor's shocked to see Steven still observing.

"Try to pay attention, Taylor. I still get paid whether you pass this module or not."

"Yes, sorry, mate... Sir."

Simon shakes his head before returning his attention to the power point onscreen.

After all eyes are definitely off him, Taylor resumes his attention to his phone. A missed call. From Simon's nan. And a text.

'Hi Taylor, just wanting 2 ask if u heard from Simon?? He didn't come home last night. Starting to get worried??? Edna X.'

Taylor bites his lip and pockets his phone. What the hell has happened to him?

Chapter Forty-Four:

"There's no way I could afford them," Sasha pouts, shelving the black shoes she had been admiring.

"Here, let me treat ya," Jennifer lifts them back up before Sasha has time to even retrieve her hand, "early birthday present."

"My birthday isn't even until October," Sasha tries, and fails, to grab the shoes back from her abnormally tall friend.

"Doesn't matter, you'll look good in them tonight. And we all know that you want to look your best for Jimmy," she teases her with the name.

Sasha smirks.

"Look, I'll throw it on the card, pay me back when you can if you want? But don't worry about it. Anyway, they'll look incredible with your dress," Jennifer's eyes light up as she trots to the counter, not taking no for an answer.

The shop assistant beams at Jennifer's approach, seeing pound signs as she spots the pile of garments slung over her arm.

"Hiya, girl."

"Hey," Jennifer scrunches up her shoulders, "nice day isn't it?"

"Lovely, wouldn't mind a jug of cocktails in the square instead of being stuck in here," the assistant giggles.

Pleasantries out of the way, the assistant bags the items as Jennifer admires the glittery pop socket hanging on display in front of the tills. She doesn't need another one. She already has five.

"So, that's £194, please."

Jennifer smiles sweetly as she roots around, pulling out a card.

"Can you throw it on this, please?"

"Of course."

"So, where are we going tonight?" Jennifer returns to Sasha as the assistant turns her back to retrieve the card machine.

Sasha was lingering to the side, feeling the material of a blouse Jennifer's sure she has three colours in. But not that one. A pale baby blue colour. Very nice, she thinks, cocking her head to the side.

"Well, after bowls I think there was talk about Levels," Sasha says, letting the blouse float back onto the hanger.

"Levels, great. Haven't been in months."

Jennifer nostalgically remembers the red heels she'd worn, and destroyed, falling down the stairs in a drunken state last time she was there.

"Sorry, miss."

Jennifer smiles back towards the assistant.

"This card was rejected, I'm afraid."

Jennifer reddens.

"Er... Sorry about that. Must be one that needs paid off. Try..."

Jennifer scrambles around in her purse. She pulls out three she knows are maxed out and groans. There's bound to be one with remaining credit on. Where's the one she got last week? She thinks it's under her mattress, cursing herself for her stupidity.

"You know what? I can go without the necklaces," she whispers with a smile at the girl, who nods before pounding her fingers against the touchscreen till.

"Everything alright, Jenny?"

"Yeah, 100%," she turns back towards Sasha with a wide grin. "Why don't you go Starbucks and get us a table? I'll have a caramel cream, cool me down," she winks.

Sasha raises her eyebrows at her, before nodding and disappearing down an aisle. Wiping the sweat collecting at the back of her neck, Jenny drums her newly done nails on the counter, biting her lip.

"That brings the total to £152."

Still too much. She doesn't have enough.

"Er... Take the skirt off too, actually."

This continues for another few moments, until Sasha's shoes are the only thing left.

"£48.98."

Jennifer jostles with her handbag, plucking out coins and trying to ignore the harsh tones from the agitated queue collecting behind her.

"Here, take these... And then pay off the rest with the credit on the card," she smiles nervously.

The assistant purses her lips, and Jennifer is relieved to hear the drum of the receipt printing once she swipes the card for the dozenth time.

"Thank you," the assistant gives a curt smile, handing over the receipt and the card, shouting *'who's next?'* before Jennifer has a chance to collect herself. Rude, she thinks, as she picks up the discarded bags and makes her way out of the shop and around the corner to the Starbucks.

"What took you so long?" Sasha thanks her as she hands over the shoebox overdramatically.

"Problems with the card. I wonder if Mum missed a payment or something... She's been going through a hard time recently with Geoff leaving and all..."

She looks down at her nails, indicating that she wants to change the subject. Luckily, it works, and Sasha starts talking about her looming poetry exam. Jennifer nods in the right places, her thoughts on the newly maxed out card resting in her denim jacket pocket. That's another one. What is she going to do?

Chapter Forty-Five:

The train ride was dodgy enough, with a homeless man patrolling the aisles like a conductor asking for spare change, so Ashley didn't have high hopes for the house. She was right, of course. The Wright's house, sitting at the end of a dingy cul-de-sac, stands alone with an overgrown lawn. As she rings the bell, she steps off the doorstep quick enough to notice a twitch in the blinds through the window on her left. She puts on her best fake smile as a shadow crosses the stained-glass square window which takes up the majority of the PVC door. She hears the click of a lock, and out steps DS Parkes. Her smile instantly drops as the detective closes the door and folds her arms.

"May I help you?"

"Er... I'm here to speak to Marie Wright."

"She never said she was expecting visitors."

Ashley scowls.

"Door stepping, then?"

"Free country, ain't it, Detective?"

"Well... I'm afraid Miss Wright is busy with me at the moment, Miss Bell."

Miss Wright?

"How about the father?"

"I'm sorry?"

Bingo! Ashley knows she's hit a nerve. She can almost see Parkes squirm.

"Where's Mr Wright?"

Parkes stutters, narrowing her eyes at Ashley. She's caught her out.

"Lee's father is not here."

"Where is he?"

"Look, Miss Bell. I don't have the time for this now. We have an ongoing investigation and right now you're wasting my time."

Ashley protests as Parkes snaps the door closed in her face. Exhaling frustratedly, she struts across the lawn and the road, turning and leaning against a lamppost in plain view in case the bitch is still watching. Bringing out her phone, she searches Matt's number and presses the phone to her ear.

"I can't talk right now, Ash."

She manages not to grimace audibly. She hates when people call her that.

"Why, what's up?"

"I'm busy chasing a lead."

"Which is?"

She hears the phone get shuffled around.

"I can't say yet."

"Even a tiny clue?" she puts on her pleading

voice, "I'm here outside the Wright's house and the sergeant won't let me in."

He sighs.

"Yeah... It's about that."

She straightens up, alert.

"Go on..."

More shuffling.

"Look," he whispers down the phone, "we're investigating the dad. He's back from living foreign and we didn't know. We don't even know if the mam knows. That's what Parkes is doing. Big boss is trying to meet with him as we speak. Turns out the lad tried to get in contact with him online a few weeks back. That's just between us, give you a head start. Nothing until it's made public, you hear me?"

Ashley reassures him whilst internally laying out her copy, pinpointing her contacts and seeing the smile on her editor's face. This just got interesting.

Chapter Forty-Six:

She was so intuitive. So boisterous and forthcoming. So unlike either of us. She was her own little character. Didn't try and mimic Mummy or Daddy, just so fiercely independent. And so, when she got sick, it hit her as hard as it hit us. Sometimes she got so frustrated when she didn't have the energy to even hold a cup of water to her lips, or when her eyes drooped and she couldn't hold a book long enough to finish a page.

We lived on that chair by her bed. The both of us. Angela and I. Taking turns to stretch our legs and get a crappy cup of coffee from the machine in the corridor down the hall. Never bothering to annoy the nurses. They had enough to do.

Liverpool General Children's Hospital was, although not too long of a drive from us, far enough away that we didn't feel comfortable leaving her alone without at least one of us at her beck and call. The nurses offered us a bed when one was free and we took turns to have a snooze whilst the other held her little hand and listened to her labored breathing.

Her mother even stopped drinking for those few weeks and months. All miscommunication and misunderstanding that had been jostled between us so aggressively throughout the years seemed to mute. Pause. Be put on standby. That is, until we heard the news that she wasn't going to make it. That opened the flood gates. We bickered in that hall for far longer than I'd like to admit. The nurses threatening that if we didn't hush that they would have to ask us to leave as we were scaring the other kids in surrounding rooms. Deciding what to do and what not to do. She was too blind sighted to see that medicines and prayers can only go so far.

No parent should ever have to bury their child. I'm sure the nurses in that hospital have uttered that phrase far too many times than they'd like to admit. It just wasn't something that happened in our everyday life. Maybe on a stupid soap that Angela used to watch whilst I made the dinner and helped our little girl with the more difficult words and sums in her homework book. Not to us. Not to a nice little family from Garston who were happy. We had a lovely two bed house. Pristine red wooden door with a window either side and symmetrical on the first floor. A tyre swing in the garden where I would push her and she would pretend she was going to fly off and land on the moon.

Like something from a picture book. Or the customary shot that rests in a photo frame in shops before you replace it with your own, less fancy and professional, one. Like a kid's drawing. Like so many of her own. Where Mummy's hands were three sticks, Daddy's head was far too big to get through the door and the crayon used for the lopsided neon green roof spilled out onto the circular window. I should've known, being in my profession especially, that it's not like that. It's never like that. Things happen. Life happens. Bad things happen to good people. These sort of things aren't reserved for pretty young actresses getting paid to shut their eyes for a few shots of them in a tiny white coffin. It does happen in real life. And it did happen... To us.

Chapter Forty-Seven:

Parking up at the Chinese restaurant, Atkins pulls his phone off the handset as he sees another incoming call from Langridge.

"Sir, we've found something else."

"Go on," Atkins nestles himself back in his seat.

"Well, we were checking through Fowlie's Facebook account. And guess what we've found? Messages from Lee."

Atkins's eyes widen.

"Really?"

"Yes, sir. Seems he tried to add him as a friend and messaged him about a fortnight ago, sending him his number and asking him if he could get in contact."

"And Fowlie?"

"Never wrote back."

"Interesting," Atkins steps out of his car and clicks the button to lock it, "get a look at Fowlie's call records. See if any contact *was* made. I'm literally in the carpark now. Couldn't send me them through in case he tries to lie his way out of this?"

"Right away, sir."

Pocketing his phone, Atkins climbs the drive up to the restaurant. As he walks in, he's greeted by a lady mopping the floors.

"No, no. We closed. Open at 12. Open at 12," she points her mop towards the sign on the door displaying the times and prices whilst trying to *'shoo'* him backwards.

"I know. I'm not looking for food. I'm looking for Kieran Fowlie."

The persistent woman's face drops when she sees the badge in Atkins's hand. She discards the mop and runs in the direction of the stairs. Moments later, down comes a man in a smart suit, but with a scraggily beard and floppy hair. Quite a contrast to his pristine checked trousers and jacket, Atkins thinks. He eyes Atkins suspiciously as he approaches.

"Mr Fowlie?"

"Yes. Detective Atkins is it?"

"Detective Inspector, yes, I-"

"I've already told you that I want nothing to do with this investigation. What has happened to Lee has got nothing to do with me. Yet you show up at my place of work badgering me? It's ridiculous. You're not going to find him cooking rice in the kitchen. I have absolutely no idea where the boy is. I couldn't even pick him out of a line up.

So, you can stop wasting your time with me. Now I'm going to have to ask you to leave."

Fowlie thunders over, his left hand outstretched and gently placed on Atkins's back, moving him forward.

"I will leave when I'm good and ready actually, Mr Fowlie."

Fowlie narrows his eyes at him and goes to speak again, but not before Atkins brings out his phone and clicks onto his emails, where the screenshots from DC Langridge have been resting.

"I thought maybe we could have a little chat about this..."

Atkins turns the screen of his phone so Fowlie has a perfect view, but it can also easily be seen by the cleaner, who is still hovering awkwardly to the side, seemingly enjoying the drama. Fowlie's face grows grave when he sees the messages, his frightened eyes resting on Atkins.

"Er..." Fowlie coughs, stepping backwards to block the cleaner's view before visibly composing himself. "Very well... I think you should come upstairs then."

Chapter Forty-Eight:

Parkes's phone blares out, interrupting the awkward silence overfilling Marie Wright's living room.

"Parkes."

"Sarge, I'm just off the phone to the inspector. I thought you should know that we've found evidence on Fowlie's Facebook that Lee was trying to make contact two weeks ago. The boss is with him now. Just to let you know in case Marie's still claiming innocence."

Parkes glares towards Marie, who is still busy blustering over the cups on the coffee table. Hopefully she didn't hear. Parkes thanks him and pockets her phone, perching herself back on the armchair by the door. When Marie returns from the kitchen and resumes herself back into the permanent groove on the sofa by the window, Parkes begins to speak.

"So... Detective Inspector Atkins is with your hus... Ex-husband now."

The news seems to shock Marie as she jolts upright.

"What? He's gone all the way to Spain?" she begins to chuckle, "I appreciate the effort, Detective. But, I really think you're chasing a false lead."

"No, actually, Marie. Fowlie isn't in Spain. He's been living near Huyton and working in a Chinese in St Helens. We think he's been home for at least five months."

Marie's mouth falls open dramatically.

"Wh... Ho... That's... No, no. That can't be. I'm sure he would've said something?"

"I thought you said you weren't in contact with him? Hadn't been since Lee was very small."

"I haven't been. But I'm sure if he was so close by that he would've at least attempted to make contact with Lee..."

Marie's hysteria melts in front of Parkes's eyes until she brings her hand to her face and looks back at the DS.

"Could he... Could he have something to do with this?"

Parkes twitches uncomfortably.

"We'll get to the bottom of it. In the meantime, we've found something that I think you might be interested in. It turns out that Lee was trying to contact his father on Facebook. Were you aware of this?"

Marie shakes her head, her whole body vibrating, as she pulls her shawl around her tighter.

"No, no. I have no idea how to use that Facebook thing. I've not even got a computer."

"And Lee didn't say anything to you about it?"

"No..." Marie stares at the photo of the two of them sitting on the fireplace, "no..."

Parkes bites her bottom lip. It seems that Marie *was* under the impression that Lee shared everything with her. This sudden revelation has proved to her that things weren't as they seemed. What other secrets will they uncover?

Chapter Forty-Nine:

The office at the top of the stairs is stifling hot, making Atkins pull at his collar instantly. Perfect interrogating conditions. Fowlie closes the door and crosses over to his desk, indicating for Atkins to retrieve the metal foldout chair in the corner. Atkins winces at the noise it makes, screeching across the wooden floor until it's level with the desk. The pair sit down and look across the impressive oak desk towards each other. Atkins glares into his eyes with one eyebrow raised slightly, determined to not break the silence. Fowlie fidgets with his cuffs and coughs before he finally breaks contact and averts his eyes towards the windows.

"So, what do you want from me?"

"What do you need to tell us?"

Fowlie snarls, reverting his eyes back.

"I have nothing of worth to say."

"On the contrary, Mr Fowlie, I think you do. Your son goes missing months after you move back into the country, a short drive away from his home, and only weeks after attempting contact. Seems a bit fishy to me, don't you think?"

Fowlie sighs.

"Why did you come home?"

"Last time I checked I didn't need to be questioned on why I moved house?"

"Just answer the question, please, Mr Fowlie."

His eyes return to the desk.

"Mam was very sick. Becky and I weren't getting on the best. She was very jealous that I had a family before. She never got over that. She was the one that made me send him cards and money. Guilt tripping me. Shortly after I stopped contact, when the boy turned 16, she became distant. Said that she was disgusted with the man I'd become. Somehow was ignorant to the fact that I moved to Spain for her and her work. I uprooted my life to move there with her. She was the woman who took me away from him. Not that Marie was overly happy when I saw him anyway. She must've been getting soft in her old age.

"Anyway, when Mam started to become unwell, I told Becky I was coming back to see her. Mam lasted until a few days after I arrived home. Obviously I stuck around for the funeral arrangements. I tried ringing Becky to tell her what happened, but she wouldn't answer. I texted and heard nothing back. So I... Just didn't go home. Got chatting to a lad at the funeral my mam knew, who owns this place. Was looking to move down south to open a new one and was looking for someone to take over as manager for him here. I ran a small café in Spain, and told him I had the experience. Came for the interview and got the job. Been living here ever since, and managing this joint."

He purses his lips and nods, his eyes distant.

"How long ago was this?"

"Well, I've been home for about six months. Mam died at the start of November. I was up and running here just before Christmas."

"And the messages?"

His soft features harden once more, memories of his lost mother long gone.

"I never use Facebook. Becky set it up for me when she got the tablet years ago, like. Thought it would be a good idea to get in contact with people I was friendly with back home. Show them how good my life had become. Pile of shit to me, to be honest. I'm not one to throw anything in anyone's faces. She tried to get me to use it a few times, but I just wasn't interested. Nosy-bastard-book, is what my Mam would call it," he says with a nostalgic smile.

"So you were unaware of Lee trying to make contact with you?"

Fowlie sighs and leans back in his chair, scratching his balding head.

"Nah, I had no idea. I've told you everything already. I spoke to the boy on the phone one

Christmas… Must be about eight or nine years ago. Anything after that was cards sent with a few notes. If he contacted me, I haven't read them. I don't use it, for Christ's sakes. Surely your contraptions at the station can see that, if you were able to bring that up?"

The pair talk a while longer before Atkins shakes his hand and leaves. When he's safely in the car once more, he rings Parkes and fills her in.

"I think I believe him, Parkes."

Parkes makes a noise for confirmation. She'd been awfully quiet throughout the whole conversation.

"What's wrong with you? Has Marie said something?"

"No, sir, she hasn't. But I do have news."

"Well, spit it out."

"There's been another missing person report. Teenage male around the same age. I think they're linked, sir."

Chapter Fifty:

"And he just never came home," Mrs Hasson buries her face in the fresh tissue plucked from her embroidered box cover.

Parkes nods and pats the lady's hand, looking over towards Atkins as he takes notes of Simon's last known movements.

"And where are Simon's parents?" Atkins questions when he's finished writing.

No subtlety.

"They don't bother with him. We took him in when he was about four-years-old. He was having an awful life up in Bootle with them. She's my daughter, and I try not to speak ill of my own flesh and blood, but when she met him... That was it. They're just two disasters together. Into all sorts. Y'know..." she brings her hand to her face and mouths the word '*drugs.*'

"And how often does Simon see his parents?"

Mrs Hasson dabs at her eyes.

"I'd say maybe once every few months. The odd Sunday after service we used to go and see them. But they were always lying in their own filth. Sometimes too far gone to even answer the door."

"I'm really sorry, Mrs Hasson," Parkes reaches for a photograph of, who she guesses to be, Simon in a school uniform, "is this a recent picture?"

"Yes, that was taken in June last when he was leaving big school. Goes to uni now, our Simon does. Can you believe it? The first in our family. We're so proud of him. His grandad would be over the moon, if he were still alive."

"Do you mind if we take a copy of this for our investigation? I mean, hopefully it doesn't go that far and he comes waltzing in now. But if we need to ask people if they've seen him, or put out a press release or hold a conference..."

Atkins and Parkes look at the pleading woman on the sofa. If this did go to a press conference, they don't know how the older lady would be able to withstand it.

"Please, please... Find him soon. If he's trapped somewhere and doesn't have enough medicine... I dread to think what will happen to him."

Atkins opens his mouth to speak but is interrupted by the doorbell. Mrs Hasson struggles to get out of her seat before Parkes marches over with a swift *'I've got it.'*

Crossing the flower-designed carpet, Parkes reaches for the door and pulls it open. She audibly gasps at who she comes face to face with. He almost trips over her in his hurry to get in through the door. It's *him!*

Chapter Fifty-One:

Has she seriously come here? Of all places. It's like she's intentionally trying to anger me. I watch her as she traipses her party in through the front doors. Their skirts like belts and their bra straps showing. I grip the wheel firmly, trying to stop myself from driving straight into them and mowing the lot of them down.

Parking down the carpark, I try to calm myself down. What a bitch. I can't go in there. Couldn't bring myself to. Who does she think she is? Trying to defy me like this? I know her little secret. It's like she knows I'm after her and has went to the one place that she knows I can't step foot in. Like a sanctuary. Pulling out my wallet, I gaze at the picture to calm myself down from having a full-blown panic attack. Very aware of the people sauntering past without a care in the world. But, sure what would they care? For all they know, I could just be sitting waiting for someone. I have to look as inconspicuous as I can.

I'll have to leave her tonight. Go and find the other one. I'll be back with a vengeance. She would do well to keep me happy. She doesn't know what I'm capable of. Well, she'll soon see.

Chapter Fifty-Two:

"Erm... Hi. Is Edna in?"

Parkes nods and steps back, letting him cross the threshold.

"May I ask how you know Mrs Hasson?"

"I'm Taylor, her grandson's best friend," he extends his hand once Parkes closes the door.

It's cold, yet clammy, Parkes notices, before he pulls away and heads for the living room. Atkins is in as much shock as Parkes is as this Taylor crosses the room and gives Mrs Hasson a huge hug, the large lady melting into the slim frame of the boy, who seems to take her weight easily. When the greeting has finished, he settles himself down beside her.

"You the police, I take it?" he eyes the detectives suspiciously.

They introduce themselves and he hovers off the sofa to shake their proffered hands.

"So, you're Simon's best friend?" Parkes says, more for Atkins's benefit than for confirmation.

"Yeah, been best mates for about five years now," Taylor nods, squeezing Mrs Hasson's hand as she lets out a soft whimper, "I was out with him last night. He went missing after we got food and he's made no contact with me since."

This can't be a coincidence, Parkes thinks. Taylor being in town at the same time and in contact with the two boys who have went missing. And why hasn't he come forward? Seen himself on the CCTV footage that was released to the public through social media yesterday. It's almost been over 24 hours.

"Did he seem strange? Off?" Atkins coughs and ignores Parkes and Mrs Hasson's probing eyes.

Parkes knows what he's getting at. But this isn't the place to do it. Not right in front of his devastated nan.

"No, not at all. He was just havin' a laugh and that with me and the boys. Then..."

Taylor fidgets.

"Go on..."

"After we got chicken, we went to see if the Hope and Anchor was still open. Down that street opposite John Moores library..."

"On the corner of the Fly in the Loaf?" Atkins nods, ignoring the not-so-subtle roll of Parkes's eyes.

"Yeah, that one! Well, we were going down there and we were just playing around... Havin' a bit of fun..."

Taylor has suddenly become very aware of Mrs Hasson's presence in the room, it seems.

"He went over to this Honda Civic and must've pressed too hard on it or something, and the alarm went off. We ran away from it, back down Hardman Street. In case the owner thought we were trying to nick his car, like. And by the time we turned around, he was nowhere to be seen. About ten minutes earlier he was saying he was thinking of going home, so when he didn't answer his phone... I just guessed that's where he went. And he hasn't been online or nothin' since."

The space grows quiet, the odd sniff from Mrs Hasson the only thing to penetrate the silence.

"Very well, Mrs Hasson. Would you like a cup of tea?" Parkes stands.

"Oh, yes. I'm so sorry, where are my manners? I'll fetch you all something now," she groans as she joins Parkes in the kitchen.

Atkins stares across the room at Taylor as he brings out his phone and sends a quick text. When Taylor sees he's being eyed, he pockets his phone and shuffles uncomfortably.

"What?"

Chapter Fifty-Three:

Her phone vibrates, threatening to topple off onto the tiled floor below as she steps out of the shower. Leah sneers at the latest message from Stuart. He must've seen her recent snap that she put as her story, asking who was heading out tonight. It is a Friday night, after all. She clicks out of the app, getting that small satisfaction that he'll see she was online and didn't open his message. He deserves it, anyway.

Crossing her room and putting her phone on charge, she gets to work on her hair and makeup. She's way too early, she hasn't even had her dinner yet. Pretty sure some of the girls aren't even back from their classes. But she likes being able to take the time to drink instead of frantically rushing to get everything done, like the other girls do. Of course, sometimes that means doing errands between the other six rooms, but she doesn't mind. Anything to make the other girls like her.

She's fitted in well here, at uni. She really panicked when Sam and her broke up and she remembered she had ticked same-sex living on the accommodation application out of fear of jealousy. She had a small group of friends back home in Leyland. Four other girls who kept themselves to themselves. They dipped in and out of the big boy's group that Sam was part of. Her other friends fancying his friends. How would she cope in a strange city where she knew no one? And in a flat full of girls? She was sure arguments and bitchiness would catch on. But so far, all of them had made really good friends with one another. She isn't overly close with Frankie, both finding it hard to make awkward small talk if they're alone in the kitchen together, but apart from that she's surprised at how easily she's adapted.

She glances at the screen of her phone as it lights up halfway through curling her hair. Him again. Stuart.

'You not speaking today?'

She grimaces again. The boy really does have no shame. Thinks with his dick. No, she'll make sure to put loads of pictures up. Just to annoy him. Show him she's having the best time without him. Even find some random boy to get a photo with. Make him jealous. Yeah... That's what she'll do, she thinks as she smirks putting on her lip gloss. Tonight will be an interesting night.

Chapter Fifty-Four:

"My mam won't be back 'til nine tonight, so should give us plenty of time," Taylor says as he flops himself down on his sofa.

The two detectives take the armchairs strategically placed in front of the TV, shuffling around slightly to see Taylor better.

"So what is this about?" Taylor says as he eyes Parkes bringing out her notepad.

"Have you seen this on social media, Taylor?" Atkins hands him over his phone, the video from the CCTV footage on a loop.

Taylor's face drops as soon as he takes the inspector's phone. He watches the screen for a few seconds longer before looking up at the pair.

"Er... What has this got to do with Simon?"

"Maybe you could tell us that, Taylor?"

He shakes his head defiantly, giving Atkins back his phone.

"I don't understand?"

"Surely you'd have seen this? It has been making the rounds on social media. Has been for the better part of yesterday and today, Taylor. The post clearly states we're looking to talk to the individuals involved and anyone else who might have witnessed this fight, or any other information. How come you haven't come forward?"

Taylor looks beside himself.

"What? Why is this going around? And yesterday? What? Simon has only been missing for a matter of hours. And it has nothing to do with that... Altercation outside the Subway. That was days ago. And Simon wasn't even there. What the f... I just don't get it?"

He looks like he's starting to hyperventilate. His eyes searching around the room frantically for answers. Parkes coughs and stands, retreats to the kitchen and comes back with a glass of water to give to Taylor. He thanks her, taking a sip as water spills down his front, his hands shaking vigorously. When he's composed himself, he places the glass on the carpet and addresses the detectives once more.

"I don't understand what's going on? Why is this video on social media?"

"How have you not seen it?" Atkins narrows his eyes at him.

"I deactivated my Facebook and Twitter account last month. I always do it coming up to exams 'cause I never get any work done. I still have the messenger to keep up with friends, and have kept Snapchat and Instagram... But I'm not on them all that often. Facebook can be very addictive. No good when you're supposed to be revising. So... If that answers your question?"

"And no one has tagged you in it? Sent it to you through messenger?"

"No, nothing. I mean, I know that it's me, so I'm not going to deny that. But others might not see a resemblance. Or maybe they're trying to protect me? I don't know. The bastard had it coming. Was rude and racist to the girl behind the counter. And when a guy stepped in to defend her... He got really agitated. Did him a favour, if you ask me. Getting in states like that and speaking to people like they're dirt. He's lucky he made it that far in the night without something happening. Anyway, why is this important? And what has it got to do with Simon?"

"That boy, Lee Wright, you are kicking in the stomach in that video," Atkins notices the wince from Taylor at the description of his actions, "has been missing since the early hours of that same morning. In fact, there has been no sightings of the boy since yourself and Adam Davies left him in the middle of Bold Street after the kickin' you gave him."

"That has nothing to do with me. I'm sure if you watch on you see me return into the Subway to my friends and get food. Once I left, he was gone. I have nothing to do with him disappearing. And I have nothing to do with Simon disappearing either, if that's what you're implying."

"Well, you are the last person to see both of these boys."

"My friends were with me that night after I went back into the Subway. And the same were with me last night when Simon left. They can vouch for me. I was with them for an hour after Simon... Well, after Simon went home, I guessed... But I guess that isn't what has happened."

"We're going to need a list of the names of these boys then, please, Mr..."

"Taylor, call me Taylor."

Atkins nods.

"Anything else you'd like to add, Taylor? Something you might not have wanted to admit in front of Simon's nan?"

Taylor fidgets, reaching for the residual water, before shaking his head.

"If you're sure?"

Taylor nods.

"Okay, if you could tell DS Parkes the full names of the people you were with last night and the night of the attack outside Subway. I'm just going to step out and make a phone call."

Atkins leaves Parkes to deal with Taylor hysterically asking how Simon and Lee can be linked as he makes for the door. He had felt the vibrations of a call in his pocket during the interview, but had chosen to ignore it. As he steps onto the street, he sees a missed call from a withheld number, and a voicemail.

"Hi, Charles. It's me... Rosie... Going to be in the bar tonight around nine... If you can pull yourself away from chasing baddies and finding missing kiddies for long enough," she giggles. "Hope to see you. If not... Sure what are the odds?"

Chapter Fifty-Five:

"Here he is," Jennifer sings as Jimmy and the boys skirt over towards them, their red takeaway trays filled with chicken wings and nachos. "What's up, lads?"

"Not a lot," Jimmy drops himself into a plastic seat beside Sasha, who tries to ignore the subtle raise in Jennifer's eyebrows, "had to wait for Danny to hurry up and do his hair. Worse than a woman."

Danny scowls, lobbing a roll of napkins at Jimmy as the group laugh along.

"Drinks?" Sasha eyes Jennifer, hopping up and sauntering over to the bar.

"He was sitting right next to you, why did you runaway straight away?" Jennifer whispers to her whilst the bartender prepares their cocktails, "you're going to give him the wrong impression."

"I can't help it, I'm so nervous," Sasha says, turning and looking at him discreetly, pretending to scan the bowling alley, "if this goes well, he could be my first boyfriend."

"Here's hoping," Jennifer winks, grabbing the drinks and running over to sit on the chair opposite from Jimmy, both to get out of paying and to leave the only vacant seat beside him.

When Sasha returns to the table, she looks concerned. Jennifer tries to ask her what's wrong by just using her eyes, but Sasha shakes her head faintly, smiling at Jimmy as he tells her a story about what they got up to last night. When the lads stand to enter the names of their party into the bowling system, Sasha throws her head forward until she's inches from Jennifer's face.

"What's up with ya?"

"Look behind me, towards the doors. Is he still there?"

Jennifer twists her head around to look behind Sasha. There is a steady amount of people both leaving and entering through the swivel doors.

"Who?"

"That man."

"What man?" Jennifer frowns.

"There was a man standing there looking in at me. Giving me a really dirty look. I'm scared, Jenny."

Only when Sasha turns around and claims he's no longer there does she settle down.

"That really spooked me, Jenny."

"You're okay. Do you know him?"

"No! That's the weirdest thing. But he does look familiar. I think I've saw him in town a few times. What if he's stalking me, Jenny?"

Jennifer laughs as if she said something funny as Jimmy returns, plonking himself down beside Sasha and wrapping an arm around the back of her chair, his other arm reaching for the plate of wings.

"What are you girls bitchin' about now?"

Sasha widens her eyes at Jennifer as she slouches back in her chair, reddening slightly when his hand drapes over her shoulder.

"Er..." Jennifer mumbles, "just about tonight. Talking about last time we were in Levels. I fell down the stairs. Made a right tit of myself."

Jimmy chuckles.

"Hope you brought appropriate shoes this time, then?"

"Your turn, Jenny," Shaun calls over after high-fiving Danny on the first strike of the evening.

"Oh, definitely," Jennifer stands and kicks her heels in the air, brandishing the signature bowling shoes that she'd been given in a size too small, "these will help me stay on my feet."

Grabbing a sparkling gold ball, she flings it down the lane, laughing along with the jeers as it swivels straight into the gutter. She stands waiting for the ball to be returned as she glances over at Jimmy talking very close to Sasha's hair sprayed hair. Sasha giggles along, but keeps jolting her gaze behind her towards the door and pulling the strap of her top over her shoulders self-consciously.

Chapter Fifty-Six:

"So... Thoughts, sir?"

The detectives sit in a carpark overlooking the River Mersey, just down from the Britannia Inn, as they take a smoke break before their return to the station.

"It depends, Parkes. Do we take the fact that both boys are estranged from members of their families as a weird coincidence?"

"Well... Not a lot of people can say they come from a simple happy family these days, sir."

Atkins grunts, thinking of the mess of his own homelife. The thought of Olivia or Michelle going missing breaks his heart. But Lee's dad and Simon's parents are beyond caring. Not fit to be parents, he thinks. His thoughts are interrupted by his phone blaring.

"Langridge?"

"Sir."

"What have you got?"

"Fowlie hasn't signed into his Facebook account in almost two years, sir."

Atkins curses.

"And no sign of that messenger app or whatever it's called on his phone or anything?"

"No, sir. Only message he's ever opened is from Becky Fowlie, who had sent him a waving GIF shortly after his account was activated."

"A waving what?"

"A waving GIF. Hard to explain, sir. Like a mini video."

Atkins grunts as he takes a drag of his cigarette.

"Also... I don't know if it'll make any difference, but I thought it strange..."

"Care to share?"

Parkes sits forward to listen attentively.

"We have had a look at the online electronic activity with Simon's phone. Messages and calls etcetera. I find it odd, but the boy downloaded a gay dating app at around six o'clock last night. He uninstalled it moments later, but we've got in touch with the app headquarters to see if we can get a copy of his conversations. The response time says to give 48 hours, but obviously we're trying to see if we can speak to someone high up to quicken the pace. Maybe that could be of significance?"

"Good going, Langridge. Anything else?"

"No, sir. DC Gregory is currently with the boy's parents. But they're wiped out of it. Don't think they're going to be very helpful."

"Keep me in the loop."

201

"Yes, sir."

"Well that's interesting," Atkins rubs his chin after he hangs up as he gazes out onto the water.

"Sir?"

"Could they be being targeted because they're both gay? For homophobic reasons?"

"There has been no evidence that Lee is gay, sir?"

"Sure he studies drama."

Parkes's head jolts back a few inches.

"And?"

"And what, Parkes?"

"Sir... With respect, just because the boy studies drama doesn't mean that he's gay. How many straight actors can you think of?"

Atkins sighs and nods his head.

"It was just a thought."

"And I'm not declining the thought, sir. I just don't think we should jump to conclusions like that and stick to facts."

"And what facts do we have, Parkes? That that Taylor boy was with both boys shortly before they went missing, but is claiming his innocence. And we have no evidence against him so are having to take his word for it. They were both in the city centre. They were both drinking. Apart from that, there's nothing. They live about 20 minutes away from each other. Didn't go to the same school. Don't even go to the same uni or college. No mutual friends or online traces of one another meeting apart from the fact they both went to Fusion Festival in 2016. There's literally nothing of worth in this investigation, Parkes. So, excuse me if I'm trying to grab onto anything that may thrust us forward to find out what the fuck is going on in this city."

Coughing and composing himself, Atkins steps out to stub out his cigarette and bin it. When he returns to the car, Parkes's face looks ashen.

"I'm sorry, sir."

"It's okay, Parkes."

He glances at the time on the dashboard. It's almost eight o'clock.

"Let's get back to the station. And get you home to that baby of yours. Relieve Callum of some duties."

"Well, I'd like to think Josh is in bed at this time," Parkes chuckles as Atkins reverses out of the space.

Truth be told, Parkes hasn't seen a lot of her son the past few days. Awake, anyway. She's only been back from her maternity leave for a month. But the thought of a suspicious suspect out there, targeting young people, has kept her up at night. Nightmares of Josh going missing driving her to slink into his room in the middle of the night and watch him sleep with tears filling her eyes. Her heart going out to Marie Wright, and tonight, she's sure, Edna Hasson.

Chapter Fifty-Seven:

It's shortly after nine by the time Atkins enters the bar inside the Hanover House. He had parked up at the station, had a quick shower and grabbed a spare pair of clothes he had shoved into the bottom of his drawer months ago. A plain white wrinkled shirt and jeans a few inches too short, but they were better than the sweaty suit he had been stuck in all day. He orders a drink from Tony and has a good look around the room, but Rosie is nowhere to be seen.

Taking his usual seat by the window, he brings out his phone to listen to the voicemail once more. She definitely said nine. Replacing the pint on the coaster, he gazes out at the revellers collecting outside Concert Square once more. Nodding to a few uniformed officers he'd know to see as they pass the window. He's glad he climbed the ranks and changed avenues so no longer has to deal with drunken fall outs and spiked girls vomiting down drains. Those weren't a fun few years. And he can imagine them to be worse now with the increase in drugs, in this city especially.

Drugs seemed to be a big deal in Lee's disappearance, but there was no mention of them last night with Simon. Maybe that's what Taylor is hiding from them? Both himself and Parkes feel like he's keeping something from them. If he recognised Atkins from his drunken stint last night, he certainly didn't mention it. It had even taken several second glances on Atkins's behalf to recognise Simon in the school picture from the shy little boy trudging after the beefy lads when he followed them into the square last night. If he had have known that something would've happened… He would've tried to keep him safe.

As he drains his drink, he stands to make his way back towards the bar. But just as he goes to stand, he sees a flash of a blue hoody. The same one Taylor was wearing today. He remembers staring at the weird logo's writing at the side of the arm. Yes, that is him. Atkins dodges behind his seat as he watches Taylor make his way up Wood Street. He decides to follow him, abandoning his seats by the window, much to the delight of a young couple hovering close by. Out he steps into the street and crosses the road, lagging back a bit and pulling the hood of his coat over his head.

He follows him through the streets before he comes to a stop just short of Pogue Mahone's. Taylor crosses the road and dodges down a side

205

street reserved for bins. Why aren't the gates locked? Atkins loses him as he steps behind a dumpster. Moments later, he reappears, Atkins pretending to be invested in a text on his phone whilst he walks by him.

Atkins watches two more people disappear down the same alley and reappear moments later, before, ten minutes after the original exchange, someone steps out and looks the street up and down. Brandishing his phone in front of him dramatically, seeming like he's searching for signal, Atkins clicks his camera icon and takes a few pictures of the man, glad that his flash was already off. When the man trudges off in the direction of Berry Street, he sends the pictures to Parkes and Langridge's emails, describing what he'd seen before pocketing his phone and making his way back down Seel Street. Who is this man? Could this be the big breakthrough the investigation needs? Time will tell.

Chapter Fifty-Eight:

I can't believe I allowed myself to be seen. I couldn't help it, the anger I had for the bitch. I watched as she laughed while ordering her drink. As she acted stupid to impress the boy whose arm she was hanging off. As she jumped up and down with her arms in the air after knocking down four skittles. *Four?* She should be embarrassed. If my little girl knew...

I lock the car as I scuttle up Slater Street. Leaving her with her friends. Safe only for tonight. She's on my list. She may enjoy the remaining time she has left. I'm deep in thought, seething with anger, as I come to one of the many crossroads and bang straight into someone coming from the street on the right.

"Oops, sorry, m-"

"Watch where you're going, mate."

My mouth drops open. What a cheeky bastard. And I recognise him, too. He throws me a dagger glare, before pulling his hood over his head tighter. It's the boy that was with him last night.

When they tried to break into my car. And the same kid that battered Lee outside the Subway the other night. What is it with this boy?

Rage flares inside me as I step out onto the road to follow him, but jump at the blare of a car horn. I step aside, waving to the driver apologetically, but as I turn, he's nowhere to be seen. Cursing, I follow the road until it branches off into a T-junction on Bold Street, right where my first victim was plucked from. I gaze at the picture of him now on the poster in the takeaway window, asking people to come forward if they have any information that could lead to his whereabouts. He looks younger there. Innocent. Probably around the same time that I started following him.

It started out harmless enough. Just curiosity. I never set out to hurt him. I never set out to hurt any of them. But after I lost her... And after I lost our last bit of connection... It must be about three months ago... Packing the car up with the bags for life from Sainsbury's, I flopped into the driver seat and fitted the key into the ignition. But something felt wrong. It didn't take long for me to realise what it was. Fingering the keyrings, I saw the loose bit of metal. The loose strand that should've held the broken heart keyring. The one that slotted into hers perfectly.

Frantically, I searched down the back of the seats and in the bags, even lifting the car mats up for good measure. I got down on my hands and knees and looked under the car. Retracing my steps throughout the carpark, where the trolleys were and up and down the aisles of the supermarket. I asked the member of staff at customer services if anything had been handed in. She just stared at me lazily, chewing her gum and shaking her head. She wasn't much older than *she* would have been. Probably just a Saturday job. Beyond caring about anything short of her paycheque at the end of the month to pay for cocktails and nights out with her friends. I cursed, banging my first on the moving belt, before rushing to my car and bursting into tears. I'd lost it. She said as long as we had it we'd always be together, no matter what... And I'd been so careless as to lose it.

After that, my mind began to wander to the other kids. That's when I had started to follow them. Wonder what they were up to. Starting off slow, like watching them leave class from the safety of my car, a newspaper in front of me and a courteous glance up... But I got addicted to it. I wanted to know where they were at all times. If they were okay. If they were up to something... That's why I'd finally cracked. Seeing Lee kicking up a fuss and starting fights, as well as taking drugs, it was enough to disgust me. A drain on limited resources, if you ask me. Did the people of this city a favour. And the boy last night? Petty theft and acting hard and butch in front of his mates. Well, that was just a nightmare waiting to happen. He'd try to be a part of them so much that he wouldn't even realise how soon it will have been before he has a rucksack full of cash and another person's blood dripping from his knife, which he swore he'd never use.

No, the world is better off without either of them. If my little girl was robbed of the opportunity to grow up and do her best, them bastards shouldn't be taking life for granted. Being stains on society. She would have excelled. She would have been top of her class. At university now, probably in London or somewhere fancy. We'd have scraped the cash together to get her the best of the best. Somehow. Whatever she wanted to do, we would have supported her. 100%.

A cough coming from beside me breaks me from my daydream, and I turn to see Angela observing me.

"Hiya, Ange."

"What are you doing here?"

Shit.

"Just meeting a few of the lads in town. A boy's leaving... Getting a transfer to Milton Keynes. Closer to home, so I agreed to meet them for a few. What about you?"

"Oh... Who's leaving?" she ignores my question.

I remember the poster behind me.

"Lee."

"I've never heard you speak about a Lee?"

"He works under me. We wouldn't be great mates, like. Wasn't even him asked me, was a few of the lads that work on my floor."

She purses her lips, seemingly satisfied with my answer.

"What about you? You look nice..."

"What?" she looks down at her summer dress, "oh, thanks. Just meeting a few of the girls, too. No fancy reason, just a piss up."

Like you would ever need a reason, I feel like saying to her. But this is good. Probably the most we've said to each other in months. We aren't fighting. I won't throw a spanner in the works.

"Good. Enjoy, then."

"You too," she nods towards me and clicks past me in her heels.

I gaze after my wife, not able to tame my eyes from glancing at her bare legs. She can still make my heart race. I long for her, just in this moment. What I wouldn't give for her to be on top of me again. Although we bickered about her drinking, the makeup sex was always the best. But after our daughter died... I can probably count on one hand how many times we've slept together. Frustrated moments of passion or obligations on our 20th wedding anniversary. Painting on fake smiles for our family and friends. Trying to ignore the fact that the most important product of our marriage wasn't there celebrating with us.

Chapter Fifty-Nine:

By the time Atkins crosses the threshold of the Hanover House, he sees Rosie bent over the bar, both elbows on the top, her mouth in Tony's ear so he can hear her order over the jeers of the other customers and the sound of the match on all the plasma screens. Atkins steals a glance at her bottom before she turns and spots him, calling him over.

"Hiya," she's sloppy and hugs him unexpectedly.

"Hi, sorry I'm late... Business," he winks at Tony as he hands him over a pint.

"Don't apologise, it must be fascinating... Your job," she smiles before pointing to a vacant table in the corner.

"I'm not sure that's the word I would use to describe it," he laughs as they sit down. "Stressful? Yes. Unexpected? Yes. But fascinating?" he lifts his hand to under his chin and pretends to be amused by a painting on the wall as Rosie laughs, sloshing a bit of drink from her glass onto the table.

"You're so funny," she giggles.

But as he raises his pint to his lips, her face drops, staring at his drink.

"What?" he turns it around to inspect it, thinking someone has spiked it or there is something in the bottom of his glass. "What's wrong?"

"You... You're married?"

Atkins glares down at his wedding ring, before attempting to slip it off with difficulty due to his hands being wet and cold from the pint. When he finally struggles it off, he brings out his wallet and pops it into his coin compartment.

"Er... I'm not, no. Well... Yes, technically I am... I'm getting a divorce."

She nods and scans the room, looking very awkward. He grabs her hand from across the table, forcing her to look back at him. She's rigid, a far cry from the overly affectionate woman mere seconds ago.

"Look... I know that sounds like a line. But I was in such a rush to get here to see you. That's why I'm dressed like a tramp," he laughs, sitting back to show her his wrinkled shirt tucked into his denim jeans. "I just forgot. I usually keep it locked in my desk drawer. Look... I probably shouldn't be telling you this... But I'm sure it'll be out soon enough, anyway. We have two missing person cases... Before that my DS was on maternity leave and I struggled with the workload as we had another disaster and another and another. I just couldn't find the time or energy to tell the guys that I was getting a divorce. So I just... Kept the ring on. During work hours, that's why it was off when you met me the other night. I just forgot tonight. I'm really sorry, and I understand completely if you'd like to leave.

"But, just so you know, I'm really interested in you. I live alone, my kids have left and live with their mother. I can only see them supervised every Saturday morning. That's how bad my marriage is... Was... There's no coming back. Kaitlyn, she doesn't work... So I'm just trying to find some way out of it without her trying to grab everything I've got. I've offered her the house, she doesn't want it. Says it has too many memories. But by the looks of things I'll have to sell it to get the money for the divorce lawyers, ones that won't bleed me dry and leave me with nothing. So, please... You're the first thing in my life that has gone right for a long time. And I know that's really weird to say after only meeting you the once. But something just clicked with us the other night. I would really like to get to know you. If you want, you can ring Kaitlyn and confirm with her, to really put your mind at rest? From what Olivia, my eldest, has been saying, it looks like she's been going on dates herself."

Rosie had sat the whole time staring into Atkins's face. Searching for insincerity. When he finally comes to a halt and sighs, his palm flat on his neck as he swivels it around, she takes his other hand.

"I believe you."

Atkins smiles.

"You do?"

"Yes. I might seem mad, but I do. And I felt it too... The other night? There's something about you. I feel like we could have a good thing going for us."

They smile towards each other as another roar from the people surrounding them draws them back into their surroundings. Atkins looks up to see Everton had scored, the footballer sliding on his knees across the pitch with his arms in the air. He rolls his eyes at the singing as Rosie giggles, her hands to her mouth.

"So, does that mean I get your number this time?"

Rosie laughs again, lifting her drink to her lips with a wink.

Chapter Sixty:

Rob Hancock reads the ten o'clock news with such confidence that she'd never be able to have. She stutters over her words even when she's alone with her Dictaphone, never mind reading live to thousands of people. Her piece edited within an inch of its short life. No wonder he's the best in the business, jumping between all local radio stations in the few years since he'd left his PR company to become a broadcast journalist. Ashley watches him through the giant glass window overlooking the studio. Aware that her segment is coming up next.

"Liverpool Police Department are still appealing for anyone who may know of anything relevant to the disappearance of Lee Wright to come forward. The boy's mother, Marie Wright, is believed to be distraught and wants her son home. His father, Kieran Fowlie, however, may not share the same grievance. Here's reporter on the ground Ashley Bell, who tried to speak with the father at his business in St Helens earlier today."

Ashley smiles as she hears her own pre-recorded soundbite takeover the airwaves, Rob flashing her a thumbs up.

"So I'm outside Wok Inn Chinese restaurant in St Helens, where Lee Wright's father Kieran Fowlie is manager. It seems Kieran was living abroad in Spain, but has recently returned to the UK. Not only that, but he has been estranged from both ex-wife Marie and son Lee for a number of years. A source has informed me that Lee had been trying to make contact with Kieran upon his return. Detective Inspector Charles Atkins has spoken to Kieran today, but left without an arrest. Gathering evidence, or a lost cause? My guess goes towards the former, as I tried to speak to Kieran earlier this evening."

The next clip surfaces, taken whilst Kieran Fowlie was physically pushing Ashley out of his restaurant, she hears him utter '*this is ridiculous*' in the background of her own probing questions.

"Why did you move home, Mr Fowlie? And what came of your son, Lee, trying to contact you? He's now missing, don't you find that strange? What have you got to say on the matter?"

A few seconds of shuffling that she decided to include as you can hear the frustration growing in Kieran's voice.

"Everything I've said, I've said to Detective Atkins. I am *not* a prime suspect. I have not been in direct contact with Lee for almost a decade.

Whatever has gone wrong in his life, or whatever has happened, has got absolutely nothing to do with me. The fact that I've returned to live in England is no one else's business but my own. I'd appreciate it if you respect my privacy. I wish the police department all the best in tracing my son alive and well, but as far as I'm concerned, I washed my hands of him years ago."

Ashley mouths the words of the last sentence, adrenaline running through her, before Rob clicks his button and resumes with other news. She knew that would light a spark in the community. People would be angry. Hopefully make him sloppy. Had she been escorted off the premises by a killer? She's unsure, but determined to stay on top of this case. Starting with contacting his wife, Becky Fowlie, in Spain.

She brings out her phone to see if she had answered her Facebook message, requesting an interview. Seeing it hadn't even been read yet, she snorts before screenshotting her page and sending it to Trixie, her helpful contact who can find the name and number of anyone with the barest of information. When the screenshot has sent, she's in the midst of sending her a cheery text asking for information at the earliest convenience when her phone lights up with Matt's number. Should she answer? She thinks not, he'll be mad at her. This wasn't made public. He might be in trouble. She doubts it, nothing he'd ever told her had come back to bite him in the ass… Yet. She'll give it a day and ring back tomorrow like nothing has ever happened.

Message sent, she clicks onto her social media platforms to see if a fuss has been kicked up about Fowlie yet. The response is as expected. People calling him a monster and a murderer. Setting up a *'Find Lee Wright'* GoFundMe page. Shunning off the Chinese, calling it a disgusting place owned by a revolting man. Lapping it all up, she almost bypasses it. A release from Liverpool Police Department's official Facebook. A boy in a school uniform grinning up at her. The post asking members of the public to come forward if they've seen him, or know of his last movements.

She almost squeals with excitement. Another boy missing? Could this be the work of a multiple murderer? What connection could this have with Lee Wright, or Fowlie? She needs to find out, as she screenshots the post, sending it to Trixie with an apology and a request to fast track this.

Clicking into her missed calls, she brings her phone to her ear as she thinks of what to say to Matt. She's in the doghouse. And she deserves it. But she needs to worm her way back into his good books. She has some grovelling to do. Another story looms, and it seems just as juicy as the last.

Chapter Sixty-One:

"So, do you have any children?"

Rosie gazes over her drink at Atkins before shaking her head.

"Probably for the best, my youngest is a little terror. We think it's the divorce. Actually bit a boy in the arm last week," Atkins laughs, "Of course, the school therapist calls it a cry for help. Not getting the attention she craves at home. She's probably right..."

Rosie nods along before changing the subject. Does she still not believe him? Atkins is sure she does, otherwise she wouldn't be still sitting here two hours later. He nods along with her story before his attention is averted to the TV screen above her, something catching his eye. The local news is on. A TV reporter stands at the top of Bold Street, up by the bombed out church, a bunch of drunk young people in the background waving at the camera and walking in and out of shot.

To her right are two pictures onscreen. One of Lee Wright, the other of Simon McLaughlin. Then it's back to the newsroom, but the subtitles are a few seconds behind, as the reporter warns people heading into town to be very vigilant, not to walk off on their own and to stay in groups. Rosie stops mid-story and turns to the screen.

"Your case?"

Atkins nods.

"Any luck with it all?"

"Nothing," Atkins takes a gulp of his drink whilst Rosie observes him. "We can't find a link. There's not even any CCTV to go on. We're basically clutching at straws for fuck sake."

Rosie shakes her head and apologises, standing to go to the bar for her round. That's when Atkins remembers the photos of the guy earlier. He brings out his phone, which he'd annoyedly put on silent when he sat down with Rosie, and sees two new emails from Langridge. He must be still at the station. Dedicated to his work, that boy, he'll give him that. He'll move up the ranks soon enough, he's sure.

'*Right on it boss, also thought you'd like to have a look at this*,' the first email said, with a link to a local news website. Clicking on it, Atkins curses. Kieran Fowlie's Facebook profile picture joined the headline '*Is father to blame for missing boy?*' Ashley Bell's by-line, of course. He shakes his head.

The second is several pictures taken from Langridge's phone of the screen in the station. Dodgy business, doing that, he thinks. He'll tell him off for it later. Rookie mistake. The pictures show the case file of a Brendan Baker, local known drug dealer. The name strikes a match of familiarity with Atkins, but he'd never put a face to the name. Never had to deal with him personally before now.

So, what does this mean? Why was Taylor seeing him so discreetly? Was he the one who Lee met during the party in Smithdown? Or was it Taylor? And did he owe them money? Did Simon get himself in a debt that he couldn't pay? Did Lee? This certainly changes things. He sends a quick message to Langridge, asking him to delete the photos straight away and congratulating him for a sound job, telling him he earned a good night sleep. The way Ashley Bell is working, he can't be too careful. Baker's face could be all over the news tomorrow morning.

Pocketing his phone, he looks up to the bar, expecting to see Rosie returning with their drinks, but she's nowhere to be seen. She must've gone to the toilet. He waits for a few moments longer, finishing his pint before standing and heading to the bar, ordering himself and Rosie one more. It takes ten minutes, and another half a pint later, before he realises she isn't coming back.

Chapter Sixty-Two:

Running through to the bathrooms, Leah just makes it to a cubicle before the vomiting starts. Tequila? What was she thinking? She knows she can't stomach shots. Never mind different flavoured tequilas. They can polish it up with nice names like bubble-gum and strawberry, but it's still tequila. And it still tastes like tequila. On the way back up especially. Even the thought of it now makes her retch again, nothing but stomach lining coming up. She's interrupted by a girl at the door knocking.

"You finished? I really need to pee, hurry up!"

Wiping vomit from her chin with her fist, Leah rolls her eyes. Standing like Bambi, she flushes the toilet and opens the cubicle door, excusing herself as she heads to the sinks. After splashing cold water over her face, she brings out her phone and opens the flat's WhatsApp group.

'*Just been violentlty ill. Fukc tequila lol. Whe4r is everyone?????*'

No one reads it. Signal's shocking in here, she's not even sure it has sent yet. She's seeing double after all. Replacing her phone in her bag, she steps out of the bathrooms and heads for the bar.

"Just a water," she shouts at the bartender.

"Vodka in your bag or what?" he winks at her.

"No, think I've had a bit too much."

She's not sure he's heard her. He brings over the glass and raises his eyebrows at her. She thanks him before gulping down the water, only to spit it all over the floor. She turns back towards him, a look of confusion on his face.

"This is vodka!"

"Well... Vodka and water, yeah."

"Why would you give me vodka and water if I just asked for water?"

"Just thought I'd give you a hand," he laughs. "Listen, I'm off on a break in 15, fancy-"

She doesn't bother to listen to the rest. She throws the glass down on the bar top, pretty sure she's spilled the lot of it, but so what? Good enough for him. Turning away and marching across the dance floor, she searches the room for her friends. There are six of them, how can one be so hard to find? Giving up downstairs, she migrates upstairs, but still no one is to be seen. Annoyed, she brings out her phone again. Her message has been delivered to Melissa and Hayley, but they haven't read it. The other four mustn't have signal.

"Fuck this!"

She sends another text to say she's leaving. As she makes it downstairs, she gives the same bartender her darkest glare before stepping out into the cold cobbled streets.

Chapter Sixty-Three:

There she is. He was sure she'd been in Greed Niteclub. He recognised the dancefloor in her snapchats. The snapchats with all the boys she was hanging out with. He messaged saying he might see her there. See if that got her talking. It didn't. Why was she ignoring him? What did he do? He was about to find out.

"I'll be back in a mo, lads," he says, dodging past the collection of people clinging to the electric heaters in the square.

Pulling his jacket collar up to protect his neck from the cold, he hurries down Wood Street. For a girl in heels, she can fairly run.

"Leah!"

She turns and spots him. He expects her to wait for him by the Italian restaurant, but she struts off again.

"Wait. Leah? Leah! What's up with ya?"

He's finally caught up with her. He goes to put his arm around her but she shrinks away from him.

"Go away, please, Stuart."

"What's the matter with ya?"

They travel up Ranelagh Street towards the Adelphi Hotel. He keeps trying to physically reach out to her, but she repeatedly pushes him away. She won't speak to him. What has he done? He must know. They pass the McDonald's, the Celtic Corner and the Walker Warrington Ale, all without her saying a word or giving any answers to his persistent questions as they climb the hill.

As they reach Hilbre Street, the entrance to her building, he finally cracks. He grabs her and pushes her against the building. Luckily, this university accommodation has over ten stories of flats, and so blocks out moonlight. All the windows bar a few are dark, lights coming from ones a good few stories high. The only thing he would have to worry about is if someone came up or down the deserted street. He has her to himself.

"What the fuck have I done, eh?"

"Stuart, please. Get off of me."

"You ignore all my texts. Ignore me in public. How do you think that makes me feel, eh? What? Rather cob off with some fat bloke instead, huh? I saw your snaps. Trying to make me jealous were you?"

She sobs, trying to pull away from him, but he shoves her back into the wall again. Pressing himself against her.

"You look fuckin' hot tonight, you know that? Really fuckin' hot. Why couldn't you have looked like this the other night? Eh?"

He pushes her head back and begins kissing her neck. She screams and thrusts her head forward, connecting with his nose. He falls back, his hand pressing against his face. Blood falls onto the ground and across his new shirt. That bitch. She runs forward towards the entrance. No, she's not getting away that easily. He pelts it after her, grabbing her arm. She screams again, pulling herself away from him with such force she collapses onto the ground, bringing him tumbling with her.

"Get off me. Stuart, get the fuck off me, now!"

He lifts his head and sees fear in her eyes. She was so vanilla the other night. Just lay there like a sack of potatoes. He should've known by their sexting. If you could even call it that. He always tried to introduce some form of dominance into their conversations, but she just shied away from it all. This really got him going. Who knew? He rests his hand on her leg and travels it up her dress, despite her kicking out at him. Just as he reaches her pants, he prepares to push inside her. She squeals once more, before he feels wind in his ears. Everything is a blur, and then he hits the ground with a hard whack. His back searing with pain.

"What the f-"

Someone had grabbed him and thrown him to the side. He looks up to see Leah still rooted to the floor, her head back and a look of horror on her face. A towering figure steps away from her and towards him.

"Go inside."

She doesn't need told twice. There's a scrabbling noise as she gets to her feet and runs towards the door. Leaving him stranded in a lonely street with this hooded figure. He swallows his nerves. Who does he think he is?

"Mind your own fuckin' business, mate."

He doesn't see the foot as it comes straight for his face until it's too late. He groans, running his tongue over the roof of his mouth. One of his teeth are loose. The fuckin' bastard. All those years of braces.

"Listen here-"

But before he can say anymore, the figure dives down on top of him, putting an arm over his head and snapping it backwards. Shoving a needle into his neck. A coldness runs through him, and suddenly everything goes black.

Chapter Sixty-Four:

The dog scurries to the front door as she hears the jingle of keys. Sure enough, it opens and her owners step into the hall.

"Hello, hello, Molly. Oh yes, did you miss us? Did you? Did you?" Grace kneels down to envelope her dog in cuddles and laughs as she licks her face.

"Alright, pups?" Harry groans as she jumps up on the sofa and prods him in the sunburnt arm, wanting attention. "There's a good girl."

"Tea?" Grace drops the suitcases in the utility room, too knackered to even think about making a start on all the washing.

"Would be great, please, love."

Grace steps through into the kitchen and turns on the light. Filling the kettle with water, she flicks on the switch as she gets a chill up her back. Stepping off the plane from sunny Salou was hard enough with their short-sleeved t-shirts and shorts, but the cold midnight air on the drive home made it so much worse and more depressing. Yet inside she still shivers. Surely the heating has been on? It should've came on at nine for an hour. She glides over and feels the radiator. It's still warm. Her body must be just extra sensitive now. Climatized to the Spanish air. As the water inside the kettle begins to bubble, she steps over to the cupboard above the island to retrieve a mug.

She hears a crunch underfoot. Lifting her sandal, she sees light glistening back up at her. Is that glass? Haunching down, she sees it is. Lifting and inspecting it, she's shocked to see it's a very big piece. Did Harry break a glass before they left? She shakes her head and places it on the island, before reaching in and bringing out two of the biggest mugs. It really is cold, hopefully the tea will warm her up. As she's filling her first cup, another glinting light draws her attention to the floor again. Another piece of glass? Thank God the kitchen door was closed or Molly could've seriously hurt herself. Surely Harry couldn't have been that careless? Sure, he finally gave into his stubbornness and has to wear glasses to read, but this is just silly.

"Harry, love?"

"Yeah?" he shouts through from the living room.

"Did you drop a glass in here before we left?"

"Did I what?"

"Drop a glass. This is the second piece I've found."

He arrives at the door, a perplexed look on his face and his bottom lip protruded.

"No, love."

"Well then what's happened?"

"Maybe the dog broke something?"

"The door into here has been closed since before we left."

"Maybe it was Violet?"

"No, Violet only ever drops food and water around for Molly, she wouldn't be snooping around our kitchen..."

"Look, there's another bit," he points over towards the French doors into the conservatory.

That's when he notices that one of the doors is ajar. Maybe that's where the chill is coming from? He thinks, goose bumps pricking his bare arms. It's blisteringly cold in there three out of the four seasons. Don't know why they bothered building one. He supposes Grace likes to sit in it and read on sunny days. He goes to shut it before he gasps, opening it further.

"Grace?"

"Yes?"

"Look..."

Stirring his tea, she brings him over his mug before compressing a squeal. The glass on the door into the conservatory from the outside is smashed. The key still hanging loosely, swaying in the breeze.

Chapter Sixty-Five:

"Pick up, pick up, pick up."

Parkes does laps of her upstairs landing, a squealing Josh in her arms.

"Hello?"

It's Ivan. This must mean Nicola's on shift. He hates answering the phone.

"Hiya, Ivan. Is Nicola in work?"

"Yeah," he yawns.

She can imagine him melting back into bed.

"She's been on the lates all this week. Why?"

There's a pause.

"Is that Josh screaming? Is he okay?"

"I don't know, Ivan. Callum's out for the night with work ones and I've convinced him I'd be okay with Josh and it's the first time I've been alone with him since I went back to work and I'm just about to fall asleep when he starts crying and crying and I thought he might need his nappy changed so I undid his vest and there's a big red rash up his back and I mean I don't know what it is, I haven't even changed his nappy in almost a full week because I've been so busy with work and the investigation and just everything's coming b-"

"Wow, wow, wow. Take a breath, girl."

Parkes exhales, tears forming in her eyes as she looks down at her baby in her arms.

"Look, it's probably normal. Our Ellie got a few bumps and rashes when she was younger and we panicked. It was always nothing to worry about. That being said, it'd be best just to get it checked. Nicola's working tonight, yes. But with it being a Friday night, it might be some wait. All the drunks in A&E, y'know?"

Parkes nods, her eyes still stinging.

"I'll page her to let her know you're on your way, okay?"

"Thanks, Ivan. But I've had a few glasses of wine. How will I get there?"

"I'm on my way."

Her heart sinks.

"Ivan, no..."

"I wouldn't have offered if I didn't want to, Lauren."

"But... But... What about Ellie? Jordan?"

"They're with their nan tonight, giving me a bit of peace."

"And I'm ruining that peace."

"I want my godson to be right as rain. I'd do anything for that little nipper."

"Honestly, Ivan. Thank you."

"No probs. I'll be there soon. And Lauren?"

"Yeah?"

"Take a break from work. Stop worrying about it and focus on your baby."

"I know. Thanks, Ivan."

Ending the call, Parkes sings and rocks Josh as she escorts him out into Callum's car, knowing the car seat is in there. When she gave birth to this little boy, she promised she would protect him. She will do anything and everything to keep her boy safe.

Chapter Sixty-Six:

He's still out cold as I pull up to the farm. Slamming my door, I trudge up to the shed and unlock it, my mind on the chainsaw tonight. Start by taking the boy's dick off, the creepy little pervert. Who knows what could've happened if I hadn't have intervened? Could the girl have fought him off? Would he have went all the way with her? Right there, in plain view of all those windows? I had taken a risk. Luckily, if anyone *was* looking down from their rooms, they only would've seen my navy jacket, hood pulled up over my head.

My head snaps up and my eyes widen. Was that the sound of a car door opening? I turn and strut down to the car. It's still there, undisturbed. I sneak to look in through the backseat, but he's just as I left him. That means it has come from somewhere else. Someone is here. What? No one is ever here. Not even during the day. I don't think I've ever actually saw another car on my trips up here. Who could it be? Was I followed? Fuck, I must've been. What the hell am I supposed to do or say if someone asks me what I'm doing here, never mind try and explain the young boy knocked out in the backseat of a stolen car?

I creep down towards the road, sticking to the shadows of the surrounding trees. The moonlight shines down on them and their branches jut out to make creepy figures on the stoned path. I step onto the grass to mask my footsteps. As I reach the road, I nestle between two bushes. Peaking my head out ever so discreetly, I look up and down the road. Still as deserted as before. Perfectly seen by the cloudless sky and the massive moon. Am I hearing things? The trees here lead onto a wood spawning for almost a mile. Behind the old house is field after field, unused since my father's retirement. There's nowhere else for a car to hide. I purse my lips and wait a few more minutes, before deeming my imagination wild and retreating back to the farm.

I reach the old well and tap it for good luck, something I did all the time as a kid before important assemblies or asking out the girl I fancied. Childish, but it always felt like it had my back. Especially now that we have shared these secrets together. It knows me better than anyone else, Angela included. I think against the chainsaw, knowing it will make too much noise and already spooked from the earlier disruption. As I step out onto the stoned path back up to the farm, I see the back door of the car lying ajar. What? I jog up and look inside. The car is empty. The bastard has escaped.

Chapter Sixty-Seven:

"Thank you so much, Nicola. I feel an utter fool."

Parkes busies herself with rebuttoning Josh's vest as her sister rips off the creased paper sheet over the bed and lobs it in the already overflowing bin.

"No problem. And don't be so silly. Er... Maybe best to just keep him in his vest for now? I know the weather has been on and off, but just make sure your house is at room temperature. Heat rashes are very common, and usually go away on their own. There are some creams you can use to soothe the pain for him, but other than that it's just a waiting game."

Parkes hides her shamed face as she pushes Josh's pyjamas to the bottom of the bag. What kind of mother is she? Surely she should be able to recognise a heat rash? She curses herself again at pressing Josh's cot against the radiator. Making a mental note to pull it back a few inches when they return home. She desperately tries to change the subject by apologising before asking how the night has been.

"Stop saying you're sorry. It could've been anything. It has put your mind to rest coming in, if anything. Oh, same old, same old. Drunk students and older men from pub fights. Typical Friday night, y'know?"

She finishes writing on the clipboard, before hanging it on the bed.

"I'll give you another few moments to get sorted."

She squeezes Ivan's arm on her way out of the room and he smiles, his eyes following her.

"Won't be long until he's good as new," Ivan blows a raspberry that makes Josh giggle as he turns back towards them.

They're just about packed away and ready to leave when Nicola returns, her face ashen.

"Nic? What's wrong?"

Panic looms in Parkes's chest, threatening to escape up her throat.

"No, nothing. Nothing. Joshy here is fine... It's just... I think you better take a look at this..."

And with that, she turns and retreats behind the solitary curtain used to give A&E patients a slither of privacy. Parkes gives Ivan a worried look, who takes squirming Josh from her arms and she follows her sister out onto the corridor thriving with people and dramas.

Chapter Sixty-Eight:

His hand over his mouth to mask his breathing seems pointless as Stuart is almost sure that his captor can hear his beating heart. He watches him examine the car, before cursing and kicking at the stones surrounding the pathway. Stuart had woken up several moments before their journey had come to a halt. He waited for him to open the door to retrieve him, set on kicking him square in the face and making a run for it. But when his crunching footsteps faded out, Stuart had peeked his head up to look through the window of the car, his head still swimming and heavy. He was nowhere to be seen.

Despite his drugged state, he knew the click of the door opening had pierced the cold night air. Swinging it back to as close to closed as he could, he resumed his original position just as he heard his footsteps returning, and seconds later, retreating again. Counting to ten, he scrambled out of the car. Where was he? He saw an old farmhouse in front of him. He had to doubletake, as he was about to go banging on the door and scream for help before thinking better of it. Would he really bring him here with witnesses so close by? It must be abandoned. Or worse... Filled with his cronies. Deciding he'd head for the trees, he had just reached the opening as he heard returning footsteps.

Now, here he sits. Nestled behind a tree. Looking out onto the clearing. His captor turning in circles, observing the scene.

"Very good," his voice is chilling as it echoes through the lonely night. "You might think you can get away from me, boy. But you can't. I grew up on this farm. I know every nook and cranny. The nearest house is miles and miles away. You might as well quit while you're ahead. Help is nowhere near close. If I were you, I would step forward and face me. Like a man."

Stuart shakes his head like he can see him, reverting his gaze behind him as he shuffles backwards as stealthily as he can. Afraid to step on a cracked twig or rustle a leaf. Anything to give away his position.

"You think you're a big man, don't you? Doing something like that to a poor and helpless girl. I'll show you a thing or two, you worthless piece of shit. I'll end you, son. Where are you? Show your face!"

He's growing agitated now, Stuart can tell. He travels deeper into the trees, the light breaking the canopy getting thinner as the branches get thicker. Surely if he continues this way, it will lead to a road? How deep can the forest be? And he very much doubts his captor knows the forest as well as he lets on. There are no distinguishing features. It's just trees and muck. He'll take his chances. Hope that he's bluffing. He never was much of a fighter.

When he gets far enough away, the clearing a mere speck in the distance, he finally turns and starts moving at a faster pace, his captor's shouts dying out the further into the trees he travels. The last thing he hears is something along the lines of *'she doesn't deserve this.'*

Chapter Sixty-Nine:

She can't stop her legs from shaking. She sobs and wipes her eyes with the back of her hand. Things could've gone worse. Way worse. But Stuart? What has happened to him? By the time the guy coming back from doing his laundry had found her, crying uncontrollably on the stairs, he said the entrance was deserted. No Stuart. No mystery man. He had phoned security, jokingly informing her that he was on good terms with them now since he had to phone them on his psycho ex who lived up the stairs from him a few months ago. Not meriting a laugh from her. How could she ever laugh again?

When security arrived, taking her shivering limbs from him, they called an ambulance that escorted her to hospital. She can't even remember the boy's name to thank him. Her trauma blocking out everything that wasn't the touch of Stuart's hand between her legs.

There's a knock on the door. Well, no. Not the door. It's a curtain. It must've been on the wall beside the curtain. She looks up to see the nurse back again with a woman in a black padded coat with Minnie Mouse pyjamas underneath.

"Hiya, Leah. I hope you don't mind... But this is my sister, Detective Sergeant Lauren Parkes. She's been in with her little boy just a few rooms away... Anyway, I think you should tell her what you've went through tonight. We aren't going to force you, of course. But I would strongly urge you to do so. To get out of your own head, more than anything, but also to make the police aware of the situation."

The police? She hadn't even considered the police. She lets out a moan, more tears coming as the two women come and sit on the bed either side of her. The nurse reaching for a tissue and the detective pulling her in for a hug.

It feels like she just lies there for hours, but it can't be more than a few minutes. She jumps as she hears a nurse with a trolley with who-knows-what thunder past. She pulls away from the stranger's embrace. Suddenly fully aware of her surroundings and her company.

"Leah, is it?"

She looks up into the policewoman's face. She has kind eyes. Leah nods, not knowing whether to trust her.

"What happened tonight, hon?"

"It wasn't my fault."

"Of course it wasn't, darling. Just please, tell me what happened."

After a few more moments of coercing and blubbering, Leah puts her head in her hands, not wanting to see either of them.

"I was seeing this boy... Stuart Busby, his name is. Well... I wasn't really seeing him, I suppose. I only met him the once. Twice... Tonight... A few days ago... He really hurt me. He was just after one thing. I'm only out of a really long relationship with my ex... I was looking for something. And I didn't get it. He used me. Just wanted sex and then didn't speak to me and wanted me to leave right away after we were done. That really upset me. So, when he started messaging again, I knew what he was after. I just didn't reply. I was walking home from town tonight and he started following me. Trying to put his arm around me and hold my hand and that. I just kept pushing him away, pleading with him to leave me alone.

"When we were walking down the street to the entrance of my flat... He went for me. Started kissing me and grabbing me. I fought him off as best as I could. But... Somehow, we ended up on the ground. He put his hand up my dress and I was screaming for him to stop. Next thing I know, this man comes and pulls him off me and tells me to go home. They're both gone. I don't know where he is. I shouldn't care, but I do. I thought I was falling in love with him... And then he done that. And he might be really hurt. Oh, God."

With that, all the fight goes out of her and she allows herself to melt into the nurse's arms. Parkes surveys her a while longer, her heart going out to her. What could she do?

"Erm... Okay, first of all... Leah. This isn't your fault. None of this is your fault. You were out enjoying your night and he couldn't take no for an answer. Believe me, this is his problem... Not yours. I'll let my team know and we can see if we can find him safe and well, and as for whoever this man is. Maybe you have him to thank for. Your guardian angel. Now, what do you say you come out and get a cup of tea or coffee, and I'll take a few more details. That sound okay?"

Chapter Seventy:

Delving deeper into the forest for a few more moments, Stuart continues to make sure not to trip on overgrowing roots and dodge under low hanging branches. Anything and everything to keep quiet. Keep safe. All he can hear is the occasional hoot of an owl. It's so quiet out here. Nothing like town. Absolutely no sign of the constant hum of traffic, banging of the flat party upstairs or screeching of seagulls fighting over dropped chips.

A snap to his left makes him halt, eyes growing wide. Pressing himself as flat as he can against the thick tree he had just crossed, he tries to open his ears for any sound of movement. Of course, it could be a fox. Or a bat. Or a bird. Anything. He's out in the sticks. But he can't be too careful. His captor's menacing voice still echoing around his head.

Who doesn't deserve this? Leah? Who is he? A family member or friend or what? Why was he following them? Or *was* he following them? Copperas Hill was definitely deserted. Not even the bar on the bottom floor of the Adelphi was open. Usually there would be middle-aged women traipsing about with their heels in their hands, trying to flag down cabs. It was even too late for them. How late had it been? What time is it now? It's far too dark to check his watch, but it's definitely late. Surely his friends should be looking for him? He's been far longer than a *'mo.'* Did anyone see him get carried away? Where was his car?

So many questions fly through his head. Questions he hopes he will get answered. If he can make it out of these woods alive. Deciding that the noise must've been an animal, he precariously twists his neck around the side of the tree. It's so dark he can barely see anything. But it looks deserted... For now. Taking a deep breath, he winces as he steps out into the open again, trying to ignore the padding his shoes make as they hit the ground.

Several more moments pass before his heart jolts. A ringtone. His ringtone. His phone! He scrambles about his trousers, trying to get it out. Fuck these skinny jeans. Finally managing to squeeze it from his pocket, he clicks ignore on the unknown number. Pressing down on the hold button, his screen waves him goodbye as it shuts down. He looks around him again. Fully alert. Who knows how much a noise like that could make in a quiet vicinity like this? He just hopes that his captor is still talking to himself in the clearing. Or went to inspect the farmhouse.

Pocketing his phone, deciding he'll turn it back on again and phone the police when he reaches the road, he looks back up and takes a step forward. But before his foot has even hit the dirt, a searing pain reverberates through his skull. Seconds later, he hears the crack. His eyes roll in his head as he sees the ground crashing down on top of him.

Chapter Seventy-One:

He really needs to change his ringtone. Fuck it's annoying. Unable to ignore it any longer, he reluctantly opens one eye. Where the hell is he? Taking a few seconds to register, he realises he's still in the hall. Slumped on the floor. He hadn't even made it to the living room last night, never mind the bedroom. Reaching for his phone, placed oddly on the first step of the stairs, Atkins sees it's Parkes. What time is it? He checks his watch and curses. It's almost half eight.

"Parkes?"

His croaky voice is still rough from sleep and the heavy night.

"Sir. Are you almost in?"

"Er..."

Atkins looks around the room, the alcohol splashing around in his stomach, threatening to escape from his mouth.

"... I'm running a little late."

"Well, hurry sir. It's urgent. There's another missing kid. I think they're linked. A boy around the same age. Went missing after getting attacked last night outside student accommodation in the city centre. We have a witness. I spoke with her last night before calling it in. Everyone's collected in the incident room waiting. I can stall for now, or do you want me to crack on?"

Atkins rests his throbbing head in one of his hands. There's no way he can drive in, he's well over the limit. He remembers that he had left his car overnight at the station anyway. He'll have to taxi it. After a shower, of course. And a gallon of mouthwash. He can still taste the ale.

"Take control of it, Parkes. I'll be there as soon as I can."

Chapter Seventy-Two:

Hanging up the phone and looking through the thin windows on the door, Parkes takes a deep breath. All eyes will be on her. She's in charge. She hopes Atkins will get here soon. Stepping through into the incident room, she smiles awkwardly as the general chatter throughout the room grounds to a halt.

"Thanks for giving up your Saturday morning, guys. But I'm sure you all know that this is a rather complex case."

She clumsily bangs her foot against the table as she crosses to the huge board. Recollecting herself, she puffs out her chest as Langridge gives her an encouraging nod.

"DI Atkins is a bit late, so until he gets here, I'll run you through what I need from you all. As we all know, Lee Wright went missing in the early hours of Wednesday morning after a night out in town. Then, in the small hours of yesterday morning, as did Simon McLaughlin. And now, we have a new name to add to that list."

Ignoring her shaking hands, she pins a picture of Stuart's face, plucked from social media, beneath the photos of the two boys she has already mentioned.

"Stuart Busby was also in town last night. He followed a girl he had previously been seeing home and things got... Physical. Luckily, someone stepped in before things got too obscene. Leah Hammond has given a statement saying that a tall man in dark clothing pulled Stuart off her at around 1:30am. He then ordered her to get inside. By the time the ambulance arrived, there was no sign of either party. I tried ringing Stuart shortly after speaking with Leah, but after a few rings, the phone got turned off. Langridge, since this seems to be your speciality, I'd like you to take control of this area of proceedings. I have sent over his details in an email."

Langridge nods, biting the top of his pen lid.

"As for what could connect these three lads, we have still come up short. Seemingly, none of them know each other, but one boy, Taylor Magee, connects both Lee and Simon. And I can almost guarantee that he has some link to Stuart as well. DI Atkins followed the boy through Concert Square last night and found him rubbing shoulders with none other than Brendan Baker."

A few tuts come from her audience, indicating that the boy needs no introduction.

"We know from first-hand accounts that Lee left his party in Smithdown to buy drugs, then got kicked out of Bangers Bar for taking them. Taylor then proceeded to attack him outside the Subway, his last known whereabouts. Taylor has deemed himself as Simon's best friend, but has been cagey with what they had gotten up to that night. Had they taken drugs? Or better yet, did Simon owe him, or Baker, money for them?

"So now, I want Stuart Busby's life picked apart. Find out everything you can about him. Did he have any run-ins with Taylor, or Baker? I can guarantee that both or one of these lads has something to do with all of this. But we need evidence, people. Last I heard, we have a man underground currently working the streets to bring Baker down. Can we get in touch with him? See if he knows anything about these disappearances? We already have Stuart's face circling social media, as well as Simon's. And the man that saved Leah from getting attacked last night... Was he a friendly onlooker? A good Samaritan? Or is he the one that took Stuart? Took Simon and Lee? I already have uniforms combing through the student accommodation, but it seems that the vast majority of the inhabitants were out enjoying a Friday night in town.

"This is going to be a shit storm, gang. But we have to embrace it. Someone somewhere knows something. It's our jobs to pick out the attention seekers from the nutjobs and find the actual cold hard facts that will bring this case to an end. Hopefully, with the three lads back home safe with their families. Any questions?"

Chapter Seventy-Three:

Knocking for the third time, Ashley starts to get restless. Is there a press conference she doesn't know about? Surely, at least one of the parents would be staying at home in case the boy returned? Exhaling frustratedly, she steps onto the unkept grass and struts over to the window. Pressing her hands either side of her face, she rests her head against the window to see in through the filthy blinds.

Through the bleakness of the living room, she turns up her nose at the disgusting mess of the room. Sure, their son is missing, and cleaning wouldn't be high up on their priority list, but the place looks like it has never seen a mop. The walls could do with a lick of paint and the stained carpet needs more than just a hoover. Takeaway pizza boxes litter the coffee table and overspill onto the floor. She sees a woman lying on the sofa, her back to the window. Behind the sofa, sitting at a pathetic circular table sits a man with one hand around a frothing pint glass and another resting on his face, his shoulders hunched over.

Growling, she marches over and starts hammering on the door. How dare they ignore her? She understands that they must be going through a lot of grief, but she's here to help. They'd do good to keep her onside. After a few moments of consistent pounding, the door swings open. There stands the man, bleary eyed and hiding in the shadows from the sun. Coughing and standing tall, Ashley smiles.

"Hi, Mr McLaughlin. I'm Ashley Bell from Radio News, Liverpool. I know this must be a very difficult time for you. I'm here because I want to help you. I want to get Simon's name out there and... And... And find him. Someone must know something. The more publicity he gets... The better chance we have of finding him."

Ashley stops talking several times as she stares at Mr McLaughlin. He just continues to look through her as if she is invisible. Ashley asks a few more questions before he slowly closes the door, despite her protests. She stands for a few more seconds on the doorstep, seemingly surprised with his reaction. Plucking out her phone, she makes her way down to the end of the drive.

"Alright, Ash?" Matt answers right away.

"Don't call me that, and what the fuck was that about?"

"What was what about?"

"I've just left Simon's parent's house. Are they socially awkward or what the hell is going on?"

She's shocked to hear him laughing down the phone.

"They're absolutely off their tits. We don't even know if they know he's missing. They haven't seen him in months, he lives with his nan. But that's what you get for going behind my back and releasing that story ya cheeky div."

Surprisingly, Ashley finds herself chuckling along. She never would've thought he would've had the balls to trick her. She deserves it, she admits.

"Okay, okay. Very funny," she rolls her eyes, "so you've sent me on a wild goose chase. Where does the boy live?"

"I'll give you one better."

Ashley stops halfway down the street, ears perked open.

"There's another boy missing. Was taken from the city centre last night, just behind Lime Street Station outside the student accommodation. And we have reason to think it's the same guy."

Chapter Seventy-Four:

Ignoring the ringtone and vibrations in his pocket, Atkins shuffles across the garden and falls into the taxi. Leaning back, wiping the sweat already glistening on his forehead, he hopes the Super doesn't hear about this. He's done well to hide the disaster of his life so far, but showing up over an hour and a half late when three young people are still missing is a cause for concern. He'll really have to think of a good excuse. His phone blares out once more and he curses, digging into his pockets to retrieve it.

"Atkins," he barks, not even bothering to check the caller ID.

"Charles?"

He widens his eyes, bringing the phone back from his ear to check that the voice registering in his head is real and not just a figment of his hungover state.

"Kaitlyn?"

"Where are you?"

"Erm... I'm on my way to work," he eyes the taxi man suspiciously. "Why, what's wrong? Are the girls okay?"

Kaitlyn avoids calling him at all costs. Even when they meet up with the kids she hardly gives any more than the curt nod and one word answers to his probing questions.

"You mean aside from being stood up by their own father? Peachy."

Slapping his hand to his head, Atkins groans. He forgot it's a Saturday morning. He should've been there to collect them a half hour ago. The social worker will surely be there taking notes with her tightly pursed lips. Fuck!

"Sorry, Kate. I've been completely snowed under wi-"

"Don't give me the same old shit, Charles. Why do you even bother with the kids anymore? You're just going to keep hurting them."

"Listen, Kaitlyn. The three boys that have gone missing, that's my case! Christ, woman, you think I have a spare second to even have dinner with a load like that on my shoulders? Look, I'll be there in 15 minutes, but I can't stay long. Like I said, I need to get into the office-"

"Do whatever you want."

And with that, she hangs up. Atkins feels like kicking the back of the seat in frustration, before he spits the new address at the driver, who raises his eyebrows at him as he indicates right.

Going to text Parkes to let her know he'll be extra late, Atkins stares at the message from the unknown number.

'Only getting my phone charged now. I had to dash last nite, I hate goodbyes lol xx. Sorry if I came across a little weird, it will just take me a while to get used to the idea of you having another life before me. I had fun though. Maybe do it again soon? R xx'

Smiling sickly, Atkins texts back right away that he'd like that. He was really annoyed and confused that she disappeared so easily last night, but he put it down to her innocence, maybe not wanting to get herself tied up in the ugliness of a divorce. He'll make it right with her, and with the girls. They're all he has left.

Chapter Seventy-Five:

"Any luck with the trace on Stuart's phone?"

Parkes brings out her own to see no new messages from Atkins. Where the hell could he be?

"Not at the minute, boss," Langridge looks up from his computer, "it's an odd one."

"Care to explain?"

"Well," he sighs, clicking onto a map of the city and scrolling up, passing Knowsley and Kirkby and Ormskirk until it rests in a patch of green area off the beaten path. "When you called him, the signal was picked up from a mast over here."

He waves his fingers in a circle around another green area, a road with a name Parkes doesn't recognise centimetres away.

"But that could cover anywhere from here," he scrolls out and indicates the left side of the screen, close to the water's edge, "to here," he repeats the procedure with the right.

"And how big of a diameter is that?"

Blowing a raspberry, Langridge nearly flinches when he looks up at the sergeant.

"Five, maybe six, miles."

Whistling, Parkes parks herself unsteadily on the corner of the DC's desk.

"It's really rural there, boss. Not a lot of use for telephone masts."

"But with Lee's phone you were able to pinpoint it right to the house in Kensington Fields, how come you can't do that with Stuart's?"

"The lack of signal is a main factor. The phone wouldn't be receiving internet, and so pinpointing its exact location is difficult unless it was hooked up to a Wi-Fi source. But as you've said, the phone has been going straight to voicemail, so I guess it has been turned off."

Parkes shakes her head, glancing around the screen at the fields and trees.

"Are there even any houses around there?"

"Not very many, sarge. My guess is he could've been on the road when you rang him, and his abductor turned the phone off, maybe threw it out the window. God knows where he could be?"

Sighing once more, Parkes stands and pats Langridge's shoulder, congratulating him before skirting over to DC Gregory.

"How about you, how are we getting on here?"

"Not much better, sarge. I contacted the mole in Baker's circle, but there hasn't been anything overly suspicious going on. Just selling. No one owing any debts or talk about raids or roughing boys up. I don't know where to go from here, if I'm honest."

You and me both, Parkes thinks. Where is Atkins? He'd know what to do. Almost as if on cue, her phone starts to ring. Excusing herself, she shifts into her office and closes the door. But when she brings out her phone, she's surprised to see it's Nicola.

"Nic, bit busy at the mo. Will have to call y-"

"No, Loz. Listen. I think I know something... I can't be sure, but I thought I'd let you know. It might be a coincidence... I don't know. But better safe than sorry. I'm on my way in, just parking at Liverpool One... I think it's big."

Chapter Seventy-Six:

She's still not home yet. I wait patiently outside her house, gazing up at her unopened bedroom window overlooking the pathetic front garden. The fresh air of the warming day still not making the rounds of the pink painted walls I can just about make out from this far down the street. Probably still out getting drunk and whoring herself out. Throwing herself over them boys who were clearly only interested in one thing.

I turn the music up a bit as that U2 song that Angela loves comes on the radio. Tapping my fingers on the steering wheel to the beat, I think back on last night. I got in really late. Later than usual. When I got up this morning, after a few restless hours of sleep, she was nowhere to be seen. Was she out of the house early, away from me? Usually she would lie in on a Saturday, especially with a hangover. Did she even make it home? Stay in one of her girlfriend's houses? Who knows? We're nothing more than roommates now. Passing each other on the way to the toilet. Me sleeping in the spare room. Not even a cover over the duvet.

What was I *really* thinking? That this would bring us closer together? Even though there's no way I can tell her what I've done. Thinking she'd almost know, sense something, and come running and thank me and our marriage would rebuild itself. We're both too blind to see that this marriage was long gone even before she was.

As the radio presenter introduces the next track, some R&B number that I don't think highly of, I see her marching up the street from my wing mirror. Her hair everywhere. Last night's clothes still on, a heel in each hand. What will her mother think of her landing home like this? Walk of shame. I almost spit out at her as she passes me, but I focus my face forward instead. She doesn't seem to notice anyway. Climbing her drive, the slam of the front door echoes throughout the lonely street, making me flinch with the impact it makes. She's the last one left. My mission is almost complete. I only need a few more hours.

Chapter Seventy-Seven:

Nicola's sitting inside the Starbucks on the bottom floor of Liverpool One when Parkes marches through the door. After ordering her mocha, Parkes plants herself at the small table opposite her sister.

"What's up, Nic? I'm really busy, I'm sure you've heard we're linking the disappearance of the two boys to the same guy who seemingly took Stuart Busby last night."

"Yeah, was leaving the hospital and saw it on the news. It's about that actually..."

Parkes gazes at her sister as she fidgets out of her jacket. It hasn't been more than nine or ten hours since she last saw her, but she looks like something huge is troubling her. Her make-up free face still beautiful and youthful even after a 12-hour shift in A&E. Parkes, herself, got about four hours last night on and off after tossing and turning. Clicking onto Stuart's social media accounts to see if there was any activity and checking and triple checking on Josh and feeling the radiator to make sure the room didn't overheat.

Callum barrelling in burping and stinking of ale at all hours of the morning didn't help. Feeling guilty now for slapping his hands off her as he tried to press himself against her, the images of poor Leah Hammond still fresh in her mind.

"I knew the name sounded familiar... Stuart Busby, that is. I just guessed he was a patient of mine a few years ago and the name sort of... Stuck. I don't know... It wasn't until I was just leaving after the end of my shift when I saw his picture on the telly. Next to Simon's and that Lee fella... I *did* treat him, both of them actually. Stuart and Simon. It was when I was back at the children's hospital. Maybe about four or five years ago. They had both just come out of major operations. That's where I know them from. I don't know if there's any relevance, but I thought I might as well say..."

Nicola sheepishly looks down at her cup as she stirs the plastic spoon wistfully, staring into the mud coloured liquid.

"You're absolutely sure?"

She looks back up at her sister with a face of surprise. She was expecting Lauren to just brush her off. Call her paranoid. Say she was looking too deeply into things, the long hours and lack of sleep catching up on her.

"I would say I'm 99.9% sure."

"And the other 0.1%, how can we find that?"

"I can see if we can get access to their medical files?"

"And you think you can do that?"

"Er... I'm not sure. I can check..."

"'Not sure' isn't good enough, Nic. I'll ring this in and try and see if we can get a warrant. This might be what we need, Nic!"

Chapter Seventy-Eight:

Pulling up to Kaitlyn's mother's house, Atkins sighs as he gazes up at its grandeur after paying the taxi. He's going to get an earful; he just knows it. But before he can even knock on the door after making his way across the grass, just to spite the old bitch, it has already flown open. He expects it to be little Michelle to greet him, but instead he's met with the disgusted face of his ex-wife.

"Kaitlyn, hi."

"You're late."

"I know," he follows her uninvitedly through into the house, "I told you work has been so busy lately."

"You smell like a brewery."

He blushes as the social worker in the living room looks up at him, her lips making her look like she's been sucking on a lemon. She has always taken Kaitlyn's side throughout this whole process.

"I went out for a few Friday night drinks, am I in the wrong profession or has that become illegal without someone telling me?"

"You can do what you like, Charles. But if you're going to find all your answers at the bottom of a whiskey bottle, at least try and be on time the next morning to collect my daughters."

"*Our* daughters, and I'm not here to collect them. Like I've said, I have to go into the office. There are three boys mis-"

"However, if you do insist on drinking the night before you collect the girls, I'd like to think you'd have the decency to not drink drive with them in your backseats, please."

She isn't listening to a word he's saying.

"I didn't drive here, Kate. And besides, it's a very quick visit, just to say hello. I need to get back and-"

Her mother walks in just then, the same look of distain on her face. Two peas in a pod.

"Hello, Charles."

"Hi, Sarah. Look, I know I'm late, but there's a perfectly reasonable explana-"

"We should be finished up just before two, just meeting Charlotte for breakfast... or should I say brunch?" she sighs, checking her watch whilst lifting her fluorescent pink designer handbag with her other hand. "We will collect the girls on our way back."

"No, neither of you are listening, I can't take them with me, I have no car. And I-"

"Well, if you must insist on staying here... I'm sure you can't get up to anything too

272

incriminating whilst Emily's here," she indicates the social worker perched on the sofa, her pen flying across the documents on her clipboard. "And the pantry is locked, with all the alcohol in it, so there's no use snooping around my kitchen looking for your next fix."

'Incriminating?' 'Fix?' He's the detective inspector of the police force, for Christ's sakes. She's treating him like a local druggie.

"I can't stay," he flounders, following them out to the garden as the lights of Sarah's BMW flash as the doors are unlocked.

Kaitlyn finally turns around.

"Well, then go, Charles. But I'm sure the court would love to know that you left your two daughters in the hands of a - probably more capable than you - social worker instead of spending the precious few hours you do have with them. We're going to meet my sister, I haven't seen her since she returned from Benidorm. Now, if you will excuse me…"

And with that, she falls into the passenger-side seat and slams the door. The engine revs its reverse and they speed off towards the main road at the start of the cul-de-sac. Leaving Atkins standing on the empty driveway, speechless.

Chapter Seventy-Nine:

Pacing the floors of the cramped office in the hospital only takes a matter of seconds, further infuriating Parkes and increasing her impatience as Nicola types away on the computer beside her. They had managed to get a warrant relatively quickly. By the time it took the pair to pack up their things and make the short drive to the hospital, in fact. Nicola greeted and hugged some old colleagues and told them why she was here and how important it was. Grateful as she was for this, as they got escorted into this office briskly, it still hasn't erased the nagging feeling in Parkes's head. What is going on? Who could be attacking kids who have had operations? What a weird motive.

"And you really can't remember what the boys were in here for?" Parkes asks for the fourth time.

If it was a similar operation, they could work from there.

"No, sorry, Loz. Like I said, it was a very long time ago and I nursed so many sick children there's only a handful I remember due to their ailments and those were only because they were so dramatic."

Parkes nods, biting her tongue. She shouldn't blame her sister and tries to compare it to herself seeing some randomer on the street and trying to remember why she arrested them five years ago. It would be almost impossible without the relevant paperwork. Working on memory alone is dangerous work. And at that, Nicola was good to remember the boy's names and faces, even after changing so much over five years. She got lucky... She hopes it's just what they need to drive this investigation forward.

The printer below the desk makes her jump, startling her when it makes a long screech as it bursts to life, spitting out page after page of, what she presumes to be, medical jargon nonsense. She's better off letting Nicola take the lead for this one.

"Right, so..." Nicola frowns as she examines the papers once she's taken them out and stapled them together, "both boys were patients here for a few weeks in October 2014. That must've been when I was treating them."

"And why were they here?"

Nicola gasps and looks up at Parkes with bulging eyes.

"What?"

"Both boys had transplants."

She looks as surprised as Parkes feels.

"What?"

"I know... How could I not remember this?"

Paediatric donations, not unlike adult donations, are very hard to come by. And the waiting list just as long. The fact that both of these boys have been targeted and received donor organs whilst in the same hospital at the same time can't be a coincidence, Parkes thinks.

"Stuart was in getting a lung transplant for..." Nicola skims the page, "... bronchiolitis obliterans."

"For what?"

Nicola screws up her eyes in thought.

"Severe damage to the lungs. Usually due to infection or injury."

"Injury?" Parkes starts pacing again, "is it possible that this was caused by his abductor? He escaped and has come back for revenge... Or to finish the job?"

Parkes's head is swimming with new ideas. Is it all starting to come together? But her enquiry is shut down with only three words from Nicola.

"I doubt it. It says here it was from an infection, and wouldn't link up with Simon's transplant."

"Which was?"

"Pancreas, the boy had dangerously low blood sugar during hypo spells. Type one diabetes," Nicola continues to scan the documents. "Apparently was very hard to bring Simon back around from these spells, and so, given his youth, he was donated a new pancreas."

That answered Parkes's unanswered questions. Thousands of people in the UK have type one diabetes and don't get new pancreases, or if they do, they'd have been on the waiting list for a long time.

"Had these spells from he started school, and he underwent surgery when he was 14. It seems both boys went under the knife on the 15th October. Stuart got his new lungs at 5am, shortly followed by Stuart receiving his pancreas three hours later."

Parkes nods before shuffling back over to the computer.

"Can you bring up Lee Wright's medical history on this contraption?"

"Contraption?" Nicola giggles, "you're starting to sound like Pops."

They both smile, remembering their grandfather, who also suffered from diabetes.

"I know. But can you?"

"If his records are on file, yeah, sure."

Several seconds of typing later, the printer flies out half a dozen more pages.

"Tell me he received donor organs too..."

Her bottom lip protruding in thought, Nicola looks up seconds later with a nod.

"Fuck!"

277

"I know... He underwent surgery to receive a new liver at 9am... Guess which date?"

"The 15th?"

"Yup."

"Fuck!" Parkes repeats.

"He had biliary atresia."

"He had what?"

Before Nicola opens her mouth, Parkes waves away her explanation.

"Let me guess, a liver disease?"

Nicola gives a soft smile as her confirmation.

"Well... Looks like we've finally found our link," Parkes sits down and whistles.

"Yup."

Nicola sighs and taps the papers off the table to line them up before slipping them into a clear file plucked from the floating shelves above their heads. Brandishing them in front of Parkes's face, she yawns.

"Right, well I'm glad I said something now then, maybe I *did* help, but I'm exhausted. Need my bed."

Parkes just stares forward, not taking in anything that Nicola's said.

"Loz? Lauren!"

Nicola snaps her fingers and pulls her out of her trance.

"Sorry, Nic. I'm just thinking... Can you find out who the donors were?"

Nicola sucks her teeth, her mouth brought over to the side and her eyes creased.

"I don't know how accessible it can be… It can be risky business. Some families of donors want to make contact months or years down the line to see how they're doing… but there's so many barricades up. They have to make requests and sometimes the outcome isn't what they hoped-"

"I understand all that, Nic. But can *we* find out?"

"Oh… Well with that warrant I don't see why not."

A few moments later, the printer spurts out a single sheet.

"You're not going to believe this."

Parkes thinks she knows what her sister is going to say. She prepares herself for the revelation.

"All of Simon, Stuart and Lee's organs were from the same donor."

Parkes slams her fist off the table, making Nicola jump.

"I knew it! I fucking knew it. Who?"

"A little girl named Lucy Marshall…"

A few clicks of the mouse later and her medical file is opened.

"She died in the early hours of that same morning from heart disease. How sad!"

Parkes shakes her head. All these children, so young and with so many health conditions. If she wasn't a nervous parent already, she certainly is now. She gets the sudden urge to go home and give Josh the biggest cuddle, but knows it's impossible. Not when she has got so much to relay to the team. Standing and grabbing her things, tutting about the state of the world, she's just about to leave when she turns to see Nicola still in her chair facing the screen.

"You coming?"

She looks up, biting her lip.

"Erm... I think there's something you should know... Lucy Marshall also donated her eyes and her kidneys. Her eyes left the hospital and were donated to the eye bank, but her kidneys didn't leave the hospital. Well... They did... But inside someone else."

Parkes gasps, realisation settling in.

"You mean..."

"She donated her kidneys to a Jennifer Jones..."

"She's next!"

Chapter Eighty:

Beeping her horn repeatedly, Ashley returns the two-finger salute the asshole driving the jeep in front of her presents her with before he speeds off left at the junction in the direction of the Baltic Triangle. Drumming her fingers impatiently on the steering wheel, she exhales with a grunt at the back of her throat. Both sides of the road are bursting with oncoming vehicles. She can't see how she'll find a way to squeeze out yet. Give her a longer drive to her destination just as long as she's not stopping and starting constantly. She hates being stuck in traffic. It infuriates her.

     The fact that Matt has been abnormally quiet doesn't help her mood. Not even texting her after he dismisses her calls, like he usually would if there was an important meeting he was attending. He knows that he should keep her onside. But since Simon's grandmother wouldn't come to the door, and nor himself or Trixie have gotten back to her with the address of the Busby's, she's been twiddling her thumbs. Itching to get at the story she knows is a corker. Her editor loved the pitch and told her to get out there and fill the copy.

Blue lights snap her out of her daydream, and she cranes her neck to see past the oncoming cars sliding onto the pavement to let a marked police car past. The sirens aren't on. Doesn't that mean it isn't an emergency? It's been over a decade since she passed her theory test, she can't be sure. But one thing she can be sure about? The car tailing the police car is owned by Detective Sergeant Lauren Parkes.

When she passes, Ashley revs her engine and speeds after her, narrowly missing another car as it honks its horn behind her. Her editor told her to do everything in her power to get what she needs, and she's not going to let him down now.

Chapter Eighty-One:

Hammering on the door, Parkes jiggles her legs apprehensively. They can't be too late. It's been... what? 11 hours since Stuart was taken? There's a cooling off period. There's *always* a cooling off period. Every fibre of her being, training and crime documentary she's ever watched screams that to her. But yet... She just doesn't feel right. She needs to get this girl police protection. And soon.

Finally, there's a shuffling sound on the other side of the door and it swings open. There stands a woman in her mid-40s, cigarette in one hand and a glass half-full of a brown liquid in the other. Her cropped hair looks dishevelled and Parkes can see an old nightie beneath the tartan dressing gown.

"Mrs Jones?"

"Yeah... Who's asking?"

Why has every one of these parents been so uncooperative? It's like the kidnapper knew what parents would be awkward to further infuriate the police. Parkes introduces herself and asks if she can come in. Mrs Jones jerks her head behind Parkes at the marked police car and its blue and red lights still flashing, a look of revulsion on her face.

"Please, Mrs Jones. This is vitally important, we need to speak to your daughter, Jennifer."

The gap in the door gets thinner as Mrs Jones goes to close it.

"She's not here. Just missed her."

Parkes sticks out her foot to stop Mrs Jones closing the door completely, wincing at the throbbing pain.

"Please, where is she?"

"Oh, I don't know. She's an 18-year-old girl for God's sakes. Could be anywhere. Probably town, girl loves her fashion. Or at a friend's, she's got enough of them. So..."

She jolts her head in the direction of Parkes's boot.

"Mrs Jones, we believe your daughter could be in danger, so please, can you tell us where she is, or can you phone her and ask her to come home right away?"

Giving Parkes a peculiar look, Mrs Jones sighs before opening the door fully, swigging from her glass and muttering an irritated *'bloody hell, come in, then.'*

Chapter Eighty-Two:

"She's not answering."

Mrs Jones, who Parkes has recently found out is called Georgia, returns the phone to the table beside her chair by the telly.

"Can you try her again?"

"She'll ring back."

"Georgia, I don't think you're understanding how important this is. We've already said we think Jennifer might be in danger. Has your daughter said anything recently about being followed or anything strange like that?"

Taking another drag from her cigarette, Georgia shakes her head, obviously bored of this conversation.

"Okay, but that doesn't mean that she's not being targeted. Where could she be? Did she just leave without saying where she was going?"

Georgia splutters a wheezy laugh.

"Of course she did. She's a grown woman, for Christ's sakes. She gives me no trouble, our

Jenny. Not like this little termite here, she's the one you'll need to watch."

She winks as she ruffles the little blonde girl's hair who is lying on the floor playing with a handheld game console. Parkes almost growls in annoyance. When Josh is older, he sure as hell won't be leaving the house without giving her a full itinerary of what he'll be getting up to.

Her own mobile blares out, making her apologise and step out into the hall when she sees Atkins's name.

"Sir."

"Parkes," he barks, "I'm sorry. I've had an absolute nightmare of a morning, but I'm on my way in now. Anything to update?"

Parkes almost snorts with amusement.

"We found out that Lee Wright, Simon McLaughlin and Stuart Busby all received donated organs in October 2014 from a Lucy Marshall. I'm currently in the home of Jennifer Jones, another organ recipient, but she's nowhere to be seen. I'm scared in case we're too late and she becomes the latest victim, but the mother doesn't seem that worried. Seems like she does this all the time."

She hears Atkins exhale over the phone.

"Blimey, Parkes. How long was I gone for?"

Parkes bites her tongue from giving her superior a sarcastic answer.

"Very good, Parkes. And the parents of the Marshall girl?"

"Sir?"

"Have you contacted them?"

Uh-oh.

"No, not yet, sir. Like I said, we just found out this information about Jennifer so rushed over here."

"Very well... Well, I say you delegate babysitting the mother to a DC, it doesn't seem like she's too worried and hopefully the girl returns later unscathed. After all, it's only been a few hours since the last kidnap."

Parkes could kiss him.

"Yes, sir."

"In the meantime, what do you say we have a chat with the Marshalls? I'm five minutes from the station, I'll find out their address and text it to you. Meet you there soon."

Bradd Chambers

Chapter Eighty-Three:

The girl was easy to grab due to her predictability. I knew when she left her front door she turned right and made her way down to the bottom of the cul-de-sac, before taking the walking lane through towards the main road. That's where it could have been a problem. She could've gone anywhere and with so many onlookers and witnesses. I had to catch her before she made it to the alley. Luckily, with it being at the very end of the street, only one house faced it. The house without a car on the driveway. Thankfully, the inhabitants were out at work or visiting family or friends. Not looking out the window as I crawled towards her in my car. A pink earphone sticking out of one ear, her attention enthralled on her phone.

"Excuse me?"

She looked up confused, her head scanning the road before finally seeing me coming to a stop. She gave a polite smile, took her earphone out and a step towards the car.

"Hiya."

"Sorry, I'm visiting my aunt and I've seemed to have gotten a bit lost."

She giggled.

"It's okay, it took me some getting used to too when we moved here. The place is like a maze. Are you looking for your way back out again?"

I nodded and she pointed behind the car.

"You want to follow the road up there then take your first right. Then it's two left turns and another right and go straight for about 30 seconds until you come to the white house with the blue door, that's when you turn right again, and then Prescot Road is right in front of you."

She beamed at me.

"So, sorry, can you say that again, but help me with these Google maps. I don't really know how to use this bloody phone."

"No probs, hon."

She took another step forward. I kept my phone rested on my lap with the app open. I knew perfectly well how to get out of there. I'd drove around that cul-de-sac dozens of times following her. But I just needed to get her as close as I physically could. The syringe filled with drugs I'd stolen from the hospital in my left hand tucked beneath my leg.

As she leaned forward to point at the screen, I smelt the strength of her perfume as her chain dangled loosely in front of my eyes. Her hair falling forward, obstructing her face from my view.

Making it easier as I shoved the needle into her neck and she slumped forward, her head in my lap. Embarrassed, I pulled her in as quickly as I could and threw her into the back seat, an old blanket covered in dog hairs shrouding her from anyone peeking into the back windows.

And now, here I am. On the way back up north to the farmhouse. My collection is almost complete. My baby girl is nearly back home where she belongs. Just a few more hours. That's all I need.

Chapter Eighty-Four:

Locking his car door behind him, Atkins sighs as he brings his vibrating phone out of his back pocket. The argument that followed Kaitlyn's return from town may have been short, but it was fiery. He doesn't know where today will leave him in terms of the future with his girls, but he has to push them to the back of his mind as he climbs the Marshall's driveway and answers the call.

"Gregory?"

"Sir. Just thought I should let you know that Taylor Magee has been arrested in the city centre for supplying class A drugs."

Coming to a halt just shy of the steps ascending to the front door, Atkins covers the phone and his mouth with one large hand.

"Thanks for letting me know, Gregory. Maybe we can get him to talk. Dangle a potential lighter sentence or immunity in front of him if he's going to cough up to something bigger. I'm sure he'll know what we mean."

"Yes, sir."

"And while you're at it…"

Atkins physically turns his body towards the oncoming traffic of the main road, hoping it will help drown out his whispering.

"See if you can connect either Taylor or Baker with Kevin and Angela Marshall, the parents of the donor. It could be worth a chase."

"Yes, sir. I've also contacted Baker's mole to keep us in the loop with anything going on on their side. With the arrest of Taylor, it could throw something in the air."

"Good work, Gregory."

"Thank you, sir. Is DS Parkes there now? I sent her through the address."

"She is," Atkins's eyes involuntarily move towards her car parked in front of his, "she must already be inside. Let me know of any progress."

Knocking on the door, Atkins turns to look at the Vauxhall Astra in the driveway. Closing in on about 10 grand, but not an overly flashy car for a surgeon and a housewife. Although Kevin did take early retirement two years ago. Maybe they downsized? After all, this small two up two down house in Belle Vale is a far cry from the one they lived in before their daughter's death. Not a suspicious thing to do after losing a child, but have they been saving up to pay someone to kill the kids who received Lucy's organs? Only one way to find out.

Hearing a key turn in the lock behind him, Atkins turns to introduce himself, his hand delving into his pocket, ready to retrieve his ID badge. But it doesn't make it that far. Once the door opens, he just stands and stares. Because right there in front of him, a shy smile on her face, is Rosie.

Chapter Eighty-Five:

Groaning lightly, Jennifer twists her neck and opens her eyes. God she's tired. What's going on? Where is she? Why is she not panicking? Is she drunk? Drugged? What happened? She can't remember what has happened. What is the last thing she can remember? Her brain should be whirling with activity, her body tensing and senses bursting into fight or flight mode. But she just lies there, trying desperately for her eyes to stay open or she'll fall back asleep again.

She stares at the white tiles above her head and goes to rub her eyes to try and keep awake. But she can't. She pouts and slowly moves her head down to the left, only to see her wrist tied to a table, the rope scaling down to a space she can't see from this angle. It's now that she realises that she's naked. Her heart should be racing, her breathing heavy, but her head just lags up and down.

Gazing around the room, she realises she must be in a garage. One side of the room shelves a plethora of tools and equipment. Right in front of her is the white garage door and to her right she sees a few petrol cans, a spare tyre and a door at the top of two steps. Where does it lead? Who brought her here? She needs to escape.

Pulling pathetically on the rope, pain sears as it digs into her wrists. Tears start to collect in her eyes, and she croaks her efforts,

"Help."

She wants desperately to scream out, but it only comes out as a whisper. Not even a whisper. She can't even hear her own attempts. Her head lolls from side to side, trying to think of, or find, anything to help. But then the door through into what she presumes to be the house clicks open and a black silhouette stands staring out at her.

Chapter Eighty-Six:

"Er... Come in."

Almost every cell in Atkins's body is screaming for him to turn and run back to the car. Drive off and not come back. What the hell is she doing here? What is *he* doing here? He almost turns and walks away, but there's something in the kindness in Rosie/Angela's eyes that makes him cross the threshold and listen to her close the door quietly behind him.

"What is going on?" he hisses at her as she crosses the hall into the living room, but shuts up when she widens her eyes and turns back towards him.

"Your colleague is already here, would you like a cup of tea Inspector..." she elongates the last letter, raising her eyebrows at him.

"... Atkins."

"Atkins. Right."

It takes a while before Atkins remembers that she had asked him a question.

"I'm fine, thank you... Angela."

Angela nods, before jerking her head in the direction of the red love seat in the corner of the room, where Parkes has already parked herself. Atkins joins her, but she doesn't meet his eye, too busy scribbling in her notebook. Does she know?

"As I was saying," Angela nestles herself into the sofa opposite them, a steaming cup cooling within her hands, "myself and Kevin haven't really been together in a few months... Years even. We still live together, but that's more out of habit. We barely even speak. I made him his favourite dinner in January for his birthday, and we sat at the dinner table and ate it together, but still didn't speak apart from polite small talk. That's the last time we've proper spent time together. We just pass by one another, living two different lives."

"So, you don't know where he is now?" Parkes narrows her eyes at her.

"Nope, I got up this morning and went to the Tesco. When I came back both him and his car were gone. Can I ask what this is about?"

"Where were you and your husband last night between the hours of midnight and 2am?"

Angela's eyes flicked towards Atkins impulsively when Parkes said *'husband,'* but only he seemed to notice. Her face starts to go red and Atkins grimaces at the situation they've found themselves in.

"I was in town. Out for drinks."

"Do you have anyone who can confirm that?"

Atkins holds his breath. Yes, *he* can. Well, for the majority of it anyway. Is she going to out him? Not that they're doing anything wrong... Are they?

"Yes."

"And your husband?"

Atkins almost sighs with relief. They know that whoever took Stuart Busby was much larger than Angela's petite frame. She couldn't have possibly carried Stuart's body unaided.

"I'm afraid I'm not sure. I did see him in town, though. On Bold Street. He said he was out for drinks with work friends for some guy who was leaving. He was a surgeon in the hospital, but retired about two years ago and we bought this place," she gestures around her. "It was too hard... Staying in that house... Too many memories," her eyes glaze over and she stares at the plug in the corner of the room.

"So, what time did your husband arrive home?"

She blushes.

"I don't know... We sleep in different beds."

She narrows her eyes at Parkes as she continues to jot down bullet points on her pad.

"Can I ask you a few questions about your daughter?"

Her face grows defiant, a frown prominent.

"Why?"

"For investigative reasons."

"What is there to investigate? She died of heart disease in 2014. There's nothing suspicious about that is there?"

"Did you ever try and find out who her organs were donated to?"

She stares at her open mouthed.

"I... No, why would I?"

"So, the name Lee Wright means nothing to you?"

"What, that lad on the telly who has went missing?"

"How about Simon McLaughlin?"

"What is this about?"

"Stuart Busby?"

"What has this got to do with me or Kevin?"

"Or, finally, Jennifer Jones?"

"Enough!"

Angela slams the cup onto the coffee table, sloshing black liquid everywhere.

"What the hell are you insinuating?"

Parkes looks at Atkins, who continues to stare at the liquid spilling onto the embroidered coasters.

"Why are you questioning me about myself and my husband and our little girl's death, and then start throwing kid's names from the news at me? Have yo-"

Angela's head snaps back a few inches as if she's been slapped.

"They... They're the ones, aren't they? That got her organs?"

Parkes looks rivetted by her notepad and Atkins doesn't take his eyes off the liquid, now inching closer to the table edge, threatening to overspill onto the fluffy white mat. Angela just stares between them both.

"This has got nothing to do with us," she jolts up and skids across the floor on her knees, level with the detective's eyes. "You have to listen to me. Believe me. We are not at fault here. We haven't exactly been happy families since Lucy's death... But that doesn't make us bad people. Murderers. Kidnappers. We're good people. We've just lost our way..."

Her eyes brimming with tears, she watches Parkes bite her pen and Atkins still not meet her penetrating gaze.

"You do believe me... Don't you?"

Parkes stands, Atkins following suit, knowing their time is done.

"Can you try and contact your husband to let him know we are looking to speak to him? Hopefully to eliminate him from our enquiries," Parkes gives the wife a fake smile before coughing and announcing their departure.

"The man's a lot of things, but he's not a murderer," Angela follows them through to the hall, still intent on pleading with them.

"We'll be in touch," Parkes smiles at her again before crossing the garden.

Atkins follows, not daring to meet Angela's dark stare.

"What you think?" Parkes whispers out of the corner of her mouth.

"I'm not sure. I kind of believe her."

Parkes nods.

"Me too, but we can't say anything until we speak with the husband. I think a tracker on his phone will do the trick."

"I don't think we have enough evidence for that, Parkes."

Why is he defending him?

"What? Sir, you can't deny that the fact that these four people have went missing after getting organs from the same donor isn't massively incriminating."

"I'm not, Parkes. But we can't just jump onboard with the dad. We need to speak to him first. I'm sure Ro... Angela is probably already warning him off if he is trouble. And if he isn't... Well then what is stopping him contacting us? I know I'd want to do that. We have to try every angle. Who were the surgeons? Nurses? There are so many other roads, not to mention how hard it would be to find out who their girl's organs were donated to. I don't know, Parkes. Something about it is fishy to me..."

Parkes looks at him frustrated.

"My sister was the nurse, *sir*," she spits the last word, before nodding and stating she'll talk to him back at the station, before crossing to her car and speeding off.

Atkins slides into his own, burying his face in his hands. How the fuck could he get himself involved in something like this? All the signs are pointing towards the Marshall's, and although Angela is married he still feels he needs to protect her. What a shit storm. He slides his fingers down his face and takes a look in the rear-view mirror towards the house to see Rosie standing at the living room window gazing out at him.

Chapter Eighty-Seven:

"Sarge?"

Parkes is so absorbed in her own thoughts that it takes Langridge three attempts to grab her attention as she walks through the room towards her office.

"Sorry, miles away."

"I think there's something you need to see."

Nestled at his desk, Langridge leans back in his chair, playing with his thumbs.

"My mam rang me earlier. Her friend Grace got back from Salou in the small hours of this morning to discover that her house had been broken into. Nothing stolen except her car."

Parkes stares at him arrogantly. She has so much going on and it seems like they're finally on the cusp of blowing this investigation open, yet he is inundating her with personal bullshit like this. She thought he was more professional than that.

"I'm sorry about that, Langridge," she says through gritted teeth, "but I think we have bigger fish to fry at the moment."

"No, I know, sarge. Please, hear me out."

Parkes sighs and returns to sitting on the corner of his desk, thoughts of an easy escape dispersed.

"So, I told her she'd have to report it missing. She said she already did but rang my mam to see if I could do anything, obviously not knowing about the missing kids as she's been away. I said to give me her number plate and I'd delegate it to the right people. But that's where it gets interesting."

A few clicks of the mouse later and grainy CCTV footage timestamped from Wednesday morning at 2:23am is wide screened on the computer.

"So, this is CCTV from the cinema on Wood Street. I reviewed it on Wednesday evening when looking for the boy, Lee. You can see him here."

He points a stubbed finger at Lee Wright tripping across the road and across Ropewalks Square in the direction of Bold Street.

"And right behind him..."

Several seconds later, a car creeps past. It's only in the camera sight for a few seconds, but enough to make out the number plate once Langridge sharpens the image.

"'GK112K?'"

"Yep," Langridge sips from his cup, "I remembered it because my sister used to do my head in back in the MSN days using '12' instead of 'R.' Looks nothing like it. But anyway, yeah. 'G KIRK' for Grace Kirkwood, naturally. But it's the number plate that made me aware of this..."

Zooming out slightly and pressing the up key on his keyboard, Parkes shakes her head as the paused footage brings the driver's face onscreen. Because staring out of the window in the direction of a retreating Lee Wright is none other than Kevin Marshall.

Chapter Eighty-Eight:

I fight with the back-door lock. I really need to fix it one of these days. Maybe it can be my next project? I grin slyly as I pull the fridge door open. Slightly different project, I'm sure. I lift the fresh carton of milk and glug a few mouthfuls. Feeling the freezing liquid migrate down my throat. Thirsty work, killing.

I misjudged how little of the drug I gave to the girl, or just took longer than usual to get myself ready. None of the others were awake once they made it onto my surgery table. It took a few blows to her head before she finally got knocked out. I extracted what I needed from her and left her there to bleed to death. Like I did the others.

Much more calming than having to inject them or cause more physical damage. I don't like what I'm doing any more than they do. But it will all be worth it. I'm nearly done. I just need to get the most important piece. Voices are carried through to me from the hall, the door through to the kitchen open just a crack. I replace the milk and sneak over, pressing myself against the door. They're coming from the living room. The TV? No... Angela... And what sounds like a man.

"Why did you lie?" the man asks.

"I didn't," Angela's crying.

I grow concerned. Is she okay? But there's something familiar about the male's voice that stops me from barging in. Is it a relative? A friend?

"You did lie, Rosie... Or whatever your name is."

Rosie? Eh? Why is he calling her by her middle name?

"I didn't, Charles."

My mind whirls trying to think of a Charles we know. A family friend's son is called Charlie, but he's only gone 11. His voice wouldn't be that deep.

"You said you didn't have any kids."

My face drops. What is going on?

"I don't, Charles. She's dead."

"And you didn't think to tell me?"

"We'd known each other... what? Two days? Look, when I was with you... I wasn't the grieving mother. The broken woman. It was like I was this new person. This better person. It was nice... I would've told you eventually. You have to believe me."

"And how uncomfortable you were when you found out about Kaitlyn. Only for me to find out that you are a married woman!"

I almost gasp. Is my wife having an affair? After everything we've been through? Is she

307

serious? I almost fling open the door and stomp into the room, but that's when I realise. The man's voice. Charles. It's Detective Inspector Atkins. I recognise his voice from the telly. Investigating the missing persons. The missing persons that *I've* taken. Has Angela grassed on me? I can't think of any other reason why he would be here. Landing me in it just to clear her guilty conscience. That fucking bitch. I'm doing all this for her. For us. Trying to bring our little girl home. And this is how she repays me? Having an affair…

  I'll show her. But I can't do it now. Not with him in the house. No, I have to get my shit together first. Show her what a mistake she's made. I'll show her exactly what I've done, I think as I close the back door as quietly as I can, before rounding the house to my car parked in the drive. I'll be the perfect husband, even if it is for a lying, cheating slag of a wife.

Chapter Eighty-Nine:

"Any updates?" Parkes shouts as she retreats from her office, her small team typing away on their computers.

"Still combing through CCTV from the nights the Busby and McLaughlin boys went missing, sarge," DC Gregory wipes sweat glistening from his brow with a napkin, "so far... No luck. Although I have collected a list of stolen cars reported the past few weeks to see if any of them were also seen around those parts."

"Keep at it," Parkes nods and pats him on the shoulder as she walks past him. "Langridge, any news?"

"I've contacted the eye bank that Lucy Marshall's eyes were delivered to. They've said nothing except she has gone on to improve four other people's vision. But without a warrant they aren't telling me anymore."

Parkes whistles.

"So, there's a chance there could be another four victims?"

"Maybe... but I don't see how Marshall could have gained access to their records. I'm struggling to see how he even could've got access to the existing victim's details."

"You're forgetting he's a surgeon. He must've found some way to access them through his work," Parkes bites her lip. "How are we on surveillance of the Marshall's house?"

"DC Crockett is currently stationed outside the house. The wife's car isn't in the drive so he's on a stakeout until either of them return."

Thanking him, Parkes tells him she'll chase up the warrant, before bringing out her phone from her back pocket. Still no answer from Atkins. Where is he? Why is he acting so strange? Sure, he loves the drink and fails to hide that well, but he can't fall through now. Not when they need him the most. They're so close.

Chapter Ninety:

Little Abbie watches as people she doesn't know shake Mummy and Daddy's hands before ruffling her hair and walking towards the carpark. She's so cold in her black leggings and just wants to go back home. And she misses Petey. It's been a long time since she last seen him. When she did, he was in that big house that smells funny filled with all those bedrooms and he had some weird straws down his mouth and up his nose. She wondered if he was getting milkshake. Because if he was then she definitely wanted some. But if he was getting some, he wasn't going to wake up for it. The past few times she had seen him he had been sleeping. If he was sleeping, then she wanted to take his milkshake too.

Then, one day they just didn't go and see Petey in the big house anymore. Mummy told her that Petey was going away and wouldn't be back. She was upset then. Thinking it was her fault. They had fallen out a few times over which toy they wanted to play with. She told Mummy that she would share all the toys and milkshakes with Petey if he would come back. Mummy just cried and hugged her, telling her it doesn't work like that and to try and get some sleep. She told her that he was up in heaven with the angels and he couldn't come back, but she would see him again someday.

But that made no sense, because she told her that he was up in heaven but then she saw him in that box in the church. The box that they had just put into the grass. She asked Mummy, who cried that his body had to stay here but his soul was going up to heaven to be with God because God kept all the souls. She doesn't know about Petey, but she wants to keep both her body and her soul here with Mummy and Daddy. She doesn't want her soul to go up into the clouds and her body to go below the grass. It's dirty down there.

Nan takes her hand just then and walks her towards the car, Mummy and Daddy following behind with the man with the white square on his t-shirt who talked for ages and ages in the church. And whenever he talked everyone cried. She didn't want to talk to him, in case she started to cry too. Looking around at all the boxes on the grass, she asks Nan why there are so many. Nan says this is where the bodies come to sleep after God takes their soul.

"What is a soul?" she asks, looking at all the different coloured boxes, crosses and statues.

"You'll find out when you're older," Nan says, a hankie pressed against her nose.

She must've been talking to that man that makes you cry again. She looks around more, wondering why people would rather be here than running and skipping and jumping and playing on the swings and slides. That's a lot more fun. She wonders if the box has food and games for the body. It must get boring down there in the dark.

When she's back in the car, the heating on and making her little toes uncurl from the cold, she asks Mummy a strange question.

"Mummy, you know the way you said Petey isn't coming back?"

"Yes, dear," she croaks pulling away from putting on Abbie's seatbelt.

"Well, what if he changes his mind and doesn't like it under the grass or up in heaven and wants to come back?"

"He can't come back, sweetheart. Once your body is under the grass, you stay there forever. But your soul lives on in heaven."

"Well, if your body stays under the ground forever, then why was that man over there digging one up? Did they change their mind? Or run out of juice?"

"What are you talking about, darling?"

"There's a man over there and he was digging at the grass."

"He was probably just burying a body with the box in it, like what they're doing now with Petey."

"No, Mummy," she rolls her eyes and crosses her arms in annoyance, "he was digging up the ways. That man was putting the grass back, this man was digging it up."

Mummy looks concerned for a moment, before telling her not to worry about it and smacking a big kiss on her forehead that will probably leave a mark from her lipstick. Closing the door, Abbie waits for Mummy to jump into the backseat beside her, but instead, she goes over to Daddy and starts whispering in his ear. They both turn towards Abbie, who waves out the window at them, before looking back in the direction where Petey's body was put into the grass. Are they changing their mind? Can he come back and play with her now? She'll even let him play with Peppa Pig, her favourite.

Chapter Ninety-One:

Coming down the stairs from Superintendent Cromby's office, Atkins fails to hide his disappointment as he runs straight into Parkes, finishing a hushed phone call in the hall.

"Sir?"

"Parkes."

Awkward silence.

"Important business?"

"What?"

He nods his head in the direction of her phone.

"Oh, no. Callum wondering when I'm coming home."

Atkins nods, averting his eyes.

"Sir... Are you okay? What has happened today?"

Atkins sighs, not wanting to get into it on the stairs. He continues down to the next floor, waving her to follow him. They collect in the empty room at the end of the corridor primarily kept for the family of loved ones giving evidence or being questioned. They settle into the comfy settees and he puts his head in his hands.

"I'm a drunk, Parkes."

Another few seconds of silence.

"Yo... You... Come on, sir. You aren't a drunk. You may like a drink, but you usually don't let it affect your work. I have smelt it off you the past few days... But it's nothing you can't come back from. You haven't done anything stupid... Coming down from the super's office... Have you?"

Atkins rubs his eyes with his hands, but still won't look up at his DS.

"I've asked to be taken off the case. Take a leave of absence."

Parkes feels like she's received a blow to the chest.

"Wh... What?"

"To be honest, I'm not in the right mind frame for any of this. I haven't been for weeks... Months even! I have been a hindrance-"

"You haven't been, sir!"

"-since the start. I saw Taylor and Simon out town the other night, the night he went missing. But I was so blind drunk I lost them in a club. Then he goes missing hours later... Everything's a mess right now."

He shakes his head and finally looks up, but stares at the minifridge buzzing in the corner. Parkes lifts a hand to pat his shoulder but decides against it and lets it fall to her side.

"Kaitlyn has left me."

Parkes blows out, seemingly surprised.

"Sir... I... I didn't know. I'm sorry."

"No one knew. Thanks, Parkes. I was seeing my kids this morning. That's why I was late. That and the fact I was hungover and either slept through my alarm or was so drunk I didn't know to set one. I have to see them every Saturday morning, whilst being surveyed by a social worker. That's how shitty my home life has been. And on top of all that, I've been on a date with Angela Marshall, the main suspect's wife of all people. It's a conflict of interest. If anyone found out about it... I would've had to have stepped down anyway. They're sending some boy in tomorrow morning from Manchester... He'll be much better than I am."

Parkes just sits and tries to digest everything he has said, the shock not settling in. They listen to the ticking of the clock and sit in comfortable silence, Atkins knowing that this is Parkes's way of showing she is there for him. But just as he's about to slap his knees and tell her to get back to work, her mobile rings, shattering the silence and ambiance.

"Parkes."

"Sarge," it's Langridge from upstairs, "quick you have to get to Toxteth Park Cemetery. As fast as you can."

"I'm downstairs, Langridge. What's up?"

"It's the girl. Lucy Marshall. Her grave. It's been dug up."

Chapter Ninety-Two:

It's been years since Ashley has followed a car like this. A chase across the docks when she was trying to get an interview with a reality star who was appearing at a local club despite being accused of paedophilia. She still gets the same thrill she did back then. She's been following the car now for a good 20 minutes. She wonders where it will stop. Where *she* will stop?

She can taste the story, right on her lips. Right within reach. The sweetness of it. And she can't wait. She needs to know what's happening. It has hooked her in. She has hooked her in. Right in. Both hands and claws. And by the looks of things, she isn't getting let go until she knows the truth. Until she knows the answers. Until she has her story and is able to shout it to the world. Luckily, she doesn't know she's following her... Yet. Probably sucked up in the drama of it all. She tries to stay one car behind anyway... Just in case. She can't lose her. And she can't lose this story.

319

Chapter Ninety-Three:

I rinse the coffee cup, adding a splash of Fairy Liquid and giving it a rub with my fingers. It's been a long time since this house has had the luxury of a sponge or washing up cloth. It's only had hot water these past few days. When I've had to wash myself, my clothes and the garage from the mess I've made. I haven't been in surgery officially in over two years, but I still find myself meticulously washing my hands. Rubbing them until they're raw. Even after only going for a piss. You don't know what you could possibly pick up. You can't be too careful.

I turn off the water and wave my hands around me to dry them, before wiping them on my trousers. That's when I hear it. The car door. It's so quiet out here that you hear everything. Is my mind imagining things? Who in their right mind would come all the way out here? Both my parents are dead, and my brother is in Asia teaching. The farm was left to me. The last time someone was out here, other than me, was when the lawyer handed me the keys after my mum's death. That was almost a decade ago.

I always said I'd sell the place. It's too isolated, I hated living here. I couldn't again. But life intervened. My job got more and more stressful and then Lucy got sick. In my honest opinion, I think I knew I'd use it sometime. Who knew that it would be for something as sinister as this?

It must be someone lost, asking for directions. That must be it. They won't have been able to see my car as it's parked around the back, but maybe they saw the farmhouse and thought they'd chance it? I cross over the white tiles into the hall and come to a rest beside the front door, the two lengthy windows either side. But it isn't someone asking for directions. And it isn't a stranger. Standing just a few feet from her car, and a few feet from the front door, is Angela. Staring through the kitchen window at the space I just vacated.

Chapter Ninety-Four:

Arriving at Toxteth Park Cemetery, the heavens open and rain starts thundering down. Cursing, knowing she has forgotten her umbrella, Parkes lifts her hood on her coat and rushes over to the crime scene. She flashes her badge at the officer at the cordon before wrestling herself under it, slipping on the wet grass. As she reaches the grave site, she asks the head SOCO what's been happening.

"Well, a man who buried his son today said that his daughter seen a man digging up a grave. By the time he went to investigate, however, Lucy Marshall's grave was deserted. But it was obvious that the grave has been tampered with. The girl died almost five years ago, and the ground looked like she had just been buried hours before. So, our boys are having a look now."

She nods her head towards the three officers appropriately attired in white jumpsuits, digging into the ground.

"I bet my left leg the bastard has planted evidence in here somewhere."

Ducking back under the barrier, Parkes clicks on Atkins's name on her phone.

"Hello," he answers.

"Sir, it's true. The grave has been tampered with. We have people digging now to retrieve what we can presume to be evidence Marshall didn't want us seeing."

Silence on the line.

"Sir?"

"Parkes, I don't want to know. I'm off the case. You don't have to answer to me anymore."

She can hear clinking and laughing in the background.

"Are you at the pub?"

"What does it matter?"

"What matters is four people have gone missing. We're starting to get a sniff at what is going on and you're at the pub?"

"I'm off the case."

"You took yourself off the case."

"Appropriately enough."

"Oh, stop feeling sorry for yourself, Atkins. Yeah, your wife left you, I'm sorry about that. But you're not going to find the answer drowning your sorrows with a bunch of hopeless cases."

Seething with anger, Parkes hangs up and texts Langridge the update, telling him to brief the team. As she makes her way back over to the crime scene, the head SOCO holds out a gloved hand.

"You might want to stand back."

"Have they found something?"

"Well... You may not have been fond of that left leg of yours."

"What? There's no evidence? Bastard! What is it then?"

"We think we've found a body."

Chapter Ninety-Five:

Angela brings the spare key out of her pocket with a trembling hand. He has to be here. She just hopes she's wrong. She twists the key in the lock and it creaks open. Stepping in out of the rain, she closes the door and stands still in the hallway, listening to her own breathing. It's so eerily quiet here. Something she never liked. When Kevin lived here, she found herself whispering in fear the whole countryside would hear her loud scouse accent. She was a proud Bootle girl through and through, there was no denying she didn't belong in a fancy farmhouse in the countryside.

She was so happy that Kevin had never tried to get her to move here, although she felt he didn't like being here either. But he has to be here, hasn't he? Where else could he be after all? All those late nights. And if she called, which she must admit wasn't very often, it would go straight to voicemail, indicating the lack of signal. She goes through into the kitchen, calling his name in a whisper. A single mug sits facedown on the counter. The living room makes her shiver at the dampness of the room that had obviously not been stepped foot in in years. The stairs creak under her weight as she checks the bathroom and three bedrooms, which are all exceptionably clean, just how Kevin's mum would've wanted, except for the thin layer of dust.

Is she wrong? Thinking the worst? But the mug... She travels back down to the kitchen and lifts it up. It's warm and still a bit wet. He must've been here. And recently. A thought crosses her mind and she looks sideways towards the door through to the garage. Could he be in there? Holding her breath, she crosses the kitchen and stands with one hand on the knob. Blowing out dramatically, she twists it, expecting to be met with a locked door. She'd never been through to the garage, or Kevin's dad's man cave, as his mother had called it. But to her surprise, the door twists with her wrist and opens sombrely.

Chapter Ninety-Six:

Pulling her car door open and falling inside, Parkes takes down her hood and turns the hot air on full blast. She melts into the seat, shivering and her teeth chattering, feeling her damp trousers stick to her legs. She presses her hands into her face and tries to block out what she's just seen.

Four bodies. Four bodies they'd pulled out of Lucy's resting place. And not one of them were hers. Of course, they still had to be officially IDed and go through post-mortem, but there was no denying the bodies were Lee Wright, Simon McLaughlin, Stuart Busby and Jennifer Jones. The SOCOs had found Jennifer's elbow first and dug around further. Lucy's coffin was still there, with the lid haphazardly shoved back on, Lee's lower half jutting out. Stuart and Simon squashed either side, and Jennifer, the most recent murder, reposing on top of them all.

All corpses were naked, with fresh stitches on their torsos. It doesn't take a specialist pathologist to know what they went through. It's safe to say that Kevin Marshall's medical cap hasn't been hung up just yet. And he's got exactly what he's wanted. Now she must ask... Where is he? And where is Lucy's body?

She sheds a tear for the four bodies as she stares at the white tent built around the scene. Still collecting evidence and taking photographs. How had she failed their families so much? It was her job to get them home safe, and now she has to tell them that their children were found buried in a shallow grave.

Chapter Ninety-Seven:

The smell hits her first. Like no smell she's ever smelt before. She almost brings up this afternoon's salad. Grabbing her blouse and scrunching it over her face, she coughs, her eyes watering, as she continues to open the door, inch by inch. She enters a spacious garage with tools hanging on the walls, nothing like what she imagined. Then again, she doesn't know what she imagined. Maybe a workstation of some sorts, Kevin's dad was always good with his hands.

She gazes around the room until she sees a large spotlight penetrating down on a table. But it's what is on the table. She gasps, unable to pull her clothes away from her face before the vomiting starts. It lashes down her front, sticking her garments to her body, before she can pull them off her face and the rest bounces off the steps. Doubling over, she retches until there's nothing left. She gasps for air, her stomach churning once again as the mouthfuls of oxygen are replaced with the rancid stench coming from the table.

Wiping her eyes, she holds the same hand over her mouth as she pulls herself to her feet, using the door for help. Because there, lying on the table, is her little girl. Lucy. She's still recognisable after all these years under the ground and wearing the pretty black dress she was buried in. The one they had selected together as a family from an online website. There are certain differences, though. Changes that show that she has been away from sunlight and love for a number of years.

Her skin is faded and dried out, almost a charcoal colour, and her hair thin and sprawled out across the table. Her face is gaunt, unlike the chubby, dimple infected cheeks she once had. And she looks... bigger? Her arms and legs definitely weren't that long. She looks stretched as if Kevin was trying to-

"Hello, Rosie."

Angela squeals, clutching at the door again for support. Turning towards the garage door, she sees Kevin step into the light from the shadows in the corner.

"Kevin," she splutters from between her fingers, her heartbeat racing, "what the fuck is going on?"

He stops about two metres from her, a white mask covering his mouth and nose, his eyes demonic like, baring into her own.

"What does it look like? I've brought our daughter home."

She steals another glance towards Lucy, and that's when she sees the candles and pictures surrounding the table. One of them in Disney World, outside the maze. Her favourite one of them at the beach, the same picture resting in a frame on their kitchen windowsill. What the hell has he done?

"Kev... I don't understand... Those kids... Why them?"

"I found them on the system in work," Kevin sighs, making her flinch as he lifts his arm, but it's just to scratch the back of his head, something he's always done when he's nervous. "I used to just lie in bed at night and think about them. Wanting to protect them. After all, a part of Lucy lives on in them. She's the reason they can run around now... Like nothing happened. Like she never even existed," he spits the last sentence, the tension in the air increasing.

"But Kev... It isn't their fault-"

"I know that, Rosie. I'm not stupid."

Why is he calling her Rosie?

"Then why them?"

"Why?" he screeches, pointing towards Lucy's corpse. "Because she would have been brilliant. She would have excelled. But instead, she gave her life for a thief... A druggie... A fraudster... A fucking rapist!"

Tears spill down Angela's cheeks now, collecting at the top of her fingers where her hand is still pressed against her mouth.

"I needed them back, Ange... I needed them back where they belong."

She gasps, looking back over towards their daughter and shaking her head.

"You mean..."

Kevin nods manically.

"Don't worry, Ange. Our little girl is back... The way she should be."

Chapter Ninety-Eight:

Tripping through his front door, Atkins throws his keys on the ground, wincing at the smack they make on the wooden floor. Wobbling through to the kitchen, he pulls open the cupboard door and reaches for the whiskey. Not even bothering to get a glass, he flops down in the chair and slugs the liquid back until it burns his insides.

Slamming it down on the table, he exhales, wiping his mouth. The world would be better without him. Letting down his girls. Ruining his chances of a reconciliation with Kaitlyn. Trying it on with a murderer's wife, who may or may not have been caught up in it. What has his life become? His phone vibrates in his pocket. He brings it out and curses when he sees Parkes's name.

Tottering out of his chair cautiously, he lobs the phone at the back wall, watching as it smashes and falls to pieces on the floor. Standing up correctly, he turns and grabs the chair. Bringing it down on the tiles several times before the legs are all he has left, one in each clenched fist. He turns and swipes everything off the table, including the whiskey bottle. When there's nothing left, he stumbles over to the counter, grabbing the toaster, the kettle, the microwave... Anything and everything, ignoring the threatening jolts as the plugs are yanked from the socket. It takes him ages to realise that he's laughing.

Moments later, when everything within his reach is lying destroyed on the floor... Only then does he let himself fall against the conservatory window and slide down onto his bottom. Curling within himself, his arms clenched around his knees, he buries his face and starts yelling, tears coming thick and fast from his scrunched shut eyes.

Chapter Ninety-Nine:

"Where's your boyfriend?"

The question throws Angela. Her eyes move back towards me. I must look crazy. Standing so calm, but with mania painted all over my face.

"Wh... What are you talking about?"

"You really think I don't know?"

I march a few steps towards her, trying to hide the pleading in my voice.

"Don't know about what?"

Roaring in frustration, I turn and grab a hammer hanging on the wall behind me. I pelt it at the garage door, getting the satisfaction of the loud thud it makes, and the aftermath of the door shuddering, like we're inside a giant bell.

"Tell me the fucking truth!"

She physically melts onto the step, shaking her head.

"There is no one else."

"Don't fucking lie to me!"

I grab a saw and chuck that at the door as well, but it's too heavy and just falls to the ground with a clamour. It seemingly does the trick, as Angela starts shaking.

"Tell me, Rosie!"

"Why do you keep calling me that?"

"'cause you really think I'm that stupid? That I didn't know you were seeing that cop," I emphasise the last word. "That you didn't rat me out!"

"I didn't."

"Stop lying to me, Angela!"

"I'm not. Yes, I... I met him the other night in the bar... And we had a drink... But I never cheated on you, you have to believe me. We didn't even kiss. And I didn't tell him anything about you. When he came to see me... I told him there's no way you could've done this. Because... Because I believed myself that you couldn't... Until I came here."

She bursts into fresh tears, shaking her head as she keeps gazing over at Lucy.

"And to think..." I creep towards her, "our daughter also gave her eyes... And they helped four people to see again."

I haunch down beside her, lifting her chin up to look into my face.

"A miracle... But in vain... As one of those people would use the gift of her eyesight to look at someone else outside the marital bed."

Chapter One Hundred:

Dusk settles as she parks up once again, bringing out her vape pen and sucking on the last remnants. It will run out of charge soon, and she hasn't got any liquid anyway. Frustrated with herself and the situation, when she runs out of juice, she rolls down the window and lets out a girlish grunt as she throws the pen out of the window, watching as it is silhouetted against the amber sky, before dropping down into the field somewhere.

Turning off the ignition and pulling up her handbrake, Parkes kicks her seat back and gazes out of the front window at the sunset. Another day gone and they still haven't caught this bastard. Naturally, Marshall's face is all over the news and social media. But with his last sighting being the little girl in the graveyard, they haven't found much else.

His mobile phone is being tracked but hasn't been turned on in hours. He hasn't used either of his cards since Saturday to take out a fifty from the ATM off Garston. She just hopes to God that he's the right man. That they're not wasting their resources and time on the wrong person. But something about the whole situation makes her know that he's guilty. His wife still hasn't returned. He was seen following Lee Wright. He has an M.O. He has access to the victim's records. Everything just makes sense.

She sighs and restarts the engine, following the direction she hopes will bring her home. She hadn't had the heart to approach each family in turn and let them know. She delegated the job to Langridge and Gregory, who went with each of the family's FLOs. She'd never had to break news like that before without Atkins. Who still hasn't answered his phone. Nor would he answer the door. And why would he? The way she spoke to him. She makes a mental note to make a point of bringing over a few drinks and his favourite pizza when this is all in the bag. Sit down and thrash it out with a proper chat. Get him back onside.

For the better part of an hour, she has been circling road after road, dipping in and out of signal on the country lanes between the coordinates that Stuart's phone last picked up signal. Like there was going to be a big sign saying: *'follow this route and we'll take you to the murderer.'* She shakes her head at her stupidity as she sees the city's lights start to flicker on in the distance. She needs to get back. She needs to get her head straight. She needs to find Marshall.

Chapter One Hundred and One:

Angela looks back up from the step, unable to hide her shock. The hand not clasped around her mouth moves towards the right side of her head, pain throbbing around her. Kevin just towers over her. His arm outstretched. His nostrils flared. His chin jutting out and tensed.

"Kevin..."

"How dare you. You didn't give a shit about her. You lay in bed hungover or drank your worries away. You never paid her any attention, even when she cried for you. Pulling at your hair and wanting you to wake up. You so fucking drunk you couldn't even register her."

Angela moans, the guilt she had buried deep within her starting to leak out.

"And even when you half-blinded yourself, you still continued to drink. How did it feel, not being able to see your own daughter grow up?

Much rather a bottle of vodka in your hand. Was it worth it? Well you can see her now, can't you?"

Grabbing for her, she squeals as he lifts her and leads her dragging feet towards the table. When she splutters again, residual vomit leaking from her mouth, he grabs her face and faces it in the direction of Lucy.

"Look at her."

She can't. She can't open her eyes.

"I said look at her!"

When she doesn't respond, he prises her eyes open and squeezes them until they hurt.

"Kevin... Please..."

"I can't find out who the other three people our little girl gave sight to were. But at least I know one person I can get her eyes from."

Realisation settling in, Angela jolts back, trying to pull herself from Lucy and Kevin standing beside her.

"Ah – no. You lost the right to her eyes when you started looking elsewhere."

Pulling her into a headlock, he moves over towards the corner of the room, where she sees a load of medical supplies.

"No, Kevin. No!"

Panic rising, she tries her hardest to pull away from him, but he has a firm grip. With his free hand, he searches the collection before bringing out a syringe.

"No!"

She starts pelting him with her fists in the stomach and groin before he releases his grip on her slightly. Turning until she is facing him, she kicks out aggressively before he finally pulls away with a *'ger-off.'* Shaking, she makes a run for the garage door.

Chapter One Hundred and Two:

Unable to ignore the muffled shouts any longer, Ashley delicately closes her car door and creeps forward. As she passes the old well, she steals a glance down it before trotting up the track. Turning to her right, she is greeted by an old farmhouse, hidden from the road by the forest surrounding it at all sides. And where Angela Marshall's car is parked.

Movement flashes across the window, making Ashley gasp and retreat into the trees behind her. From the darkness, she watches as Angela Marshall thunders out of the front door and around her bonnet until she jumps into her car. But despite starting her engine, she doesn't move. That's when Ashley notices her tyres, they're completely flat. All four of them. Angela clambers out and curses when she notices this too, before heading straight in Ashley's direction.

Ashley presses herself against the old oak, as Angela thunders past her, in too much of a hurry to even notice her surroundings. What is she running from? And in such a rush? What happened her car? Ashley must know. Making sure the clearing is deserted, she trots across to the car. The tyres have been slashed. What is going on? She approaches the front door, flinching at the crunching of the stones below her feet. Peering in at the darkened house, she climbs the steps and places a foot in the cold hallway. Wrapping her cardigan around her tightly, she looks up the stairs at the moonlit landing, before moving further into the house.

The living room on her left is uninhabited, which leaves the kitchen to her right. Where the window overlooks Angela's car. Stepping through into the old-fashioned room, she gazes around at the giant Aga which takes up one side of the room. She notices the single mug on the draining board, and then the door ajar through to what she presumes to be the garage. Whatever has made Angela flee will surely be in there.

As she crosses the kitchen, she scrunches up her face. What on earth is that smell? She tries to contain her cough and her presence, pulling her top over her face and nose, blinking through her watering eyes. When she's almost at the door, it is flung open and a figure comes barrelling out towards her. Screaming as it launches itself on her, she falls backwards and hits her head off the counter.

Chapter One Hundred and Three:

Her phone blares out as she reaches the bottom of the hill. Meticulously reaching and pressing the handsfree button, Parkes begs for it to be some news.

"Parkes."

"Sarge," Langridge's voice booms over the speaker, "we've found something."

Parkes punches the air and woops.

"Hit me with it, Langridge."

"We've been trying to contact you, where have you been?"

"I've been searching the country roads where Stuart's phone last had signal, but I'm almost back in the city now."

"Well, you may turn back around because we have an address."

"You *what?*"

"It's Marshall's parent's place. It's been desolate now for about seven years since both of

345

his parents passed away suddenly within a few months of each other. But our records show that it has been left to Marshall in their will… And it's right within the phone triangulation from the Busby boy's phone last night. I'll send the address through now and uniforms and I are on our way. We were just waiting for the green light from you, boss."

Cursing, Parkes yanks her steering wheel to the right and screeches her car into a U-turn. When she straightens up, she pulls to the side, barking her confirmation, ignoring the pang of guilt she got from being called *'boss.'* Within seconds, the address is on her phone and she types it into her maps. Clicking into street view, she recognises the old redbrick well she had passed only an hour ago. She still doesn't see a house as the dirt track snakes its way into the trees.

"I've got ya. I've fucking got ya," Parkes laughs, pushing her gearstick into first and speeding off, tyres spinning, back in the direction she came.

Chapter One Hundred and Four:

Grumbling and mumbling incomprehensively, I close the front door after one last look around. I'm upset I'm not able to complete the set, but at least I'll be able to finish it on my terms. God knows where she could be now. She could've taken the road. She could've taken either side of the forest. Wherever she is, I don't have much time. Checking that lady's purse, I see from her ID that she's a local radio journalist. If the likes of her are sniffing around, then the police won't be too far behind.

Pulling the garage door in from the kitchen closed, I turn and study the journo's car. After slashing Angela's tyres, I knew there was no way of using hers. And she's blocking the side of the house from bringing around my own. I'm just lucky that I found the journalist's car out on the roadside and decided it would be useful. I've parked it in the garage, the headlights shining on my little girl. I meander around it now, attaching a funnel to the exhaust, lucky it's the same shape. I pop the other end of the funnel into the back-seat window, before closing it as far as I can without stopping the flow through the funnel. Sighing, I press a kiss into my hand and rest it on my little girl's head, before jumping into the front seat. Pushing the seat back to get comfortable, God she's tiny, I twist on the ignition. The car splutters to life, pushing the fumes from the exhaust through the funnel and into the window open behind me. I clutch the keyring in my fist, determined not to lose this one. I felt bad taking it from her grave, but we are going to be reunited soon. I want to give it to her as a peace offering. As an apology for losing mine. I hope she'll understand. Now all I have to do is wait.

Chapter One Hundred and Five:

As the dizziness descends and the sickness takes hold, I just clutch the steering wheel, my eyes clouding over as I gaze onto the table where the remnants of my little girl rest. It was so hard digging up her grave. I cried as soon as I started shovelling and was blinded by the tears when it hit the tiny white coffin. Of course, being underground for so long, I knew retrieving her wouldn't be easy. To stop her falling apart, I wrapped her in her favourite pink blanket, before placing her in my boot. After looking around and seeing no one looking my way, I tipped the four bodies into the grave, useless now that I'd got what I wanted from them, before replacing the earth over them.

Despite my best efforts, as I lay her on the table, bits of her limbs started to peel off. I put them back as best as I could, and replacing her organs was an easy job as the skin was so thin. I could've used a teaspoon to cut through her, my surgical knife deemed worthless. Seeing her brought back all the repressed memories. Her lying

349

in the hospital bed, always wanting to be sitting up even when she was too exhausted. Her tiny voice pleading with me, begging for me to help her. Me? A surgeon. Most of my life spent in a hospital, and I could do nothing to help my little girl when she most needed me. Her eyes glazed over. Angela's eyes.

Even before she actually got the operation, they had the same eyes. Angela developed several ailments from her years of excessive drinking. Her eyesight deteriorating included. Whenever Lucy fell sick, Angela could barely see out of her left eye, her right completely useless. When she got given her sight back from parts of Lucy's transplant, I thought maybe it would give her an epiphany. That she'd somehow stop drinking and we could be a family again. There for each other after little Lucy was put into the ground.

Of course, that was wishful thinking. The only thing to come from the operation was the fact she didn't need my help anymore, despite relying on me to help her with the majority of life's skills for a number of years prior. Like having an infant in the house again. She went out with her friends and came back at all hours, even when I had work the next day.

I moved into the spare bedroom in our new house almost instantly, deeming her late nights the reason. But the truth? I could barely look at her. When I presented the question of moving house, she just agreed without any further discussion or argument. Showing how little she cared. Well, to hell with her, I think, as my eyes start to close over. She can live the rest of her life in denial and guilt. But I've done everything I could. I brought my little girl home.

I can feel myself slipping away. Although I'm finding it hard to breathe, my fist clenched at my chest, I feel relaxed. The most relaxed I've felt in years. A white light engulfs me, and I look around, trying to figure out where I am. I see a black dot in the distance and strain my eyes to see better. I don't have the energy to get up and walk towards it, but it's getting bigger. It's coming this way. Surely, I should be scared? But I just know it's going to be okay. And true enough, whenever the dot comes into view, I can see it's Lucy. A smile breaks my face, the first genuine one in months. She floats towards me, her milky teeth beaming at me. I feel tears creep down my face. She's just as I remember her. When we're within touching distance, I reach my right arm out towards her. She opens her mouth.

"Kevin!"

Chapter One Hundred and Six:

Coughing and spluttering, though from the mess on the table or the fumes, she's unsure. Parkes shuts off the engine and pulls Kevin out of the car. He's a very heavy and well-built man, so she struggles. A few times she strains to lift him by his waist. She's too weak. Finally, she manages to pull his torso and drop him out of the car. He lands with a crack on the garage floor.

"Kevin! Kevin? Can you hear me?"

She presses her head against his chest and feels his pulse. It's faint, but it's there.

"C'mon. Wake up, man."

She begins CPR. Compressing his chest repetitively and pressing her face against his mouth to feel for breath.

"No, no, no, no."

Blowing into his mouth several times, she presses on his chest desperately. Not now, not when she's so close. She knows what he's done is awful, and it takes all of her energy and curiosity to leave the mess on the table for now... But she needs to get him back. He needs to stand trial. Face up to what he's done. This is the easy way out. His victim's families wouldn't want this. And she doesn't want this.

She's just about to move down to perform mouth to mouth once more, when she gasps. His eyes are open, and he gazes up at her with a small smirk on his face. He's alive.

"Kevin? Kevin, can you hear me? My name is Lauren, Lauren Parkes. I-"

The rest of her introduction is lost as she receives a blow to her head and a ringing in her ears. She falls on her front to splat her head off the garage floor. Shouting his rights, she twists around to pull herself up, but he's on top of her, pinning her to the ground with his knees. All she can see is the garage door.

"Kevi-"

His head is right beside hers. His arms wrapped around her throat and mouth. She struggles, kicking out, but can't reach him. Her arms useless next to her. She screams and screams, but they are muffled with the great man's arms. She feels his rancid heavy breath on her face. No, this won't be the last thing she sees. The last thing she feels. She shakes her head, trying to headbutt him, but he manoeuvres his head out of harms way. Her feet still won't connect with anything and her arms throb with the pain of the heavy man digging into them. She must try anything and everything to get him off. Anything and everything to save her life. But, eventually, the fight starts to run out of her. Her energy depletes. Her muscles relax. Her eyes glaze over and she can't struggle anymore.

Chapter One Hundred and Seven:

Where is she? She rummages around in the blackness of the trees. Tripping over roots. Banging into branches. Scratching her face and her hands. Not caring. Just wanting to get out. She's been running in circles. She just knows it. There's no way she can still be in the forest. It feels like she's been running for hours. The light of the moon barely breaking the canopy of the trees above.

Then she hears them. Faintly at first, but they grow louder. Sirens coming from her right. Without thinking or caring, she makes a break for it. Sprinting in the direction of their wails. Moments later, when the trees become thinner and more sparsely placed, she begins to see the red and blue lights bouncing through the darkness towards her. Thank God.

But just as she jolts around one tree, she comes face to face with a figure. Stifling a scream, she looks up into her husband's face. Clearly terrified and panting. They stare at each other for a few seconds, the unspoken apologies and obvious years of pain and hurt bouncing between them like a movie screen. Clearing her throat as they hear voices carried towards them, she steps back and stretches out her left arm. As if she were holding a door open for him. Nodding, tears in his eyes, he begins to run again. She feels the cool air drift past her, and when his footsteps have subsided, she takes a long breath in before continuing her journey towards the farmhouse, the flashing lights and safety.

Chapter One Hundred and Eight:

Atkins has been seated in his car for a little over five minutes now, with no plans on moving anytime soon. He watches as Callum returns from the site, Josh in his arms and Ivan and Nicola either side of him. Little Josh squirming to be let down. At least the little boy will know his mummy was brave and killed in the line of duty. He hadn't known what to say, he had just shaken their hands and his head. They understood.

But what they won't ever understand is how he feels for not being there. Ignoring her calls and not answering the door. Too involved in his own shit. Something he'll never be able to forgive himself for. He had already attended Stuart's funeral yesterday, with Simon's later today, followed by Lee's and Jennifer's later in the week. He wasn't looking forward to any of them. But he had gotten the hardest one out of the way at least. Parkes's. His partner's.

For the past two weeks, he has been housed up on his own. Drinking the days and his guilt away. His only visitor Superintendent Cromby, who had given him a bollocking for taking a leave of absence at such a critical time. For keeping his emotions buried about his divorce until it was too late. She never said anything, but Atkins knew as he watched her drive away that she blames him for Parkes's death. That she believes it should've been him.

Marshall was caught, thankfully. Days after the initial search. 20 miles north of his childhood home in a Tesco Express trying to pay for food with shrapnel. He thought the hood would suffice, but luckily a woman with a new-born baby noticed him from social media and called it in. The fight was out of him by that time, and he sang like a bird when questioned. His lawyer says he'll plead guilty to five accounts of murder, so at least he won't put the families through a horrendous trial, especially considering the states they found the bodies in.

He's brought back to the present by seeing a familiar face. Ashley Bell. Talking to DC Gregory a few yards away. He shakes his head. After everything that has happened that woman, you'd think she would give it a rest. Is being resuscitated after being tied up by a murderer in the back of your own gas-filled car not enough to knock you off your feet for a while? *'Drugged By Dr Kevin Marshall: The Daddy Who Went Crazy.'* That's what her first-person feature piece in the paper had been called. A two-page spread about how she had been captured and could've been one of the murder victims. He's glad the families saw through her claim to fame and slammed their doors in her face countless amount of times.

But yet here she is again. Hounding another police officer. But wait... What? DC Gregory has leaned in for a hug, and plants a kiss on the top of her head. Could it be? The inside information all these years? The details about his life and divorce and fall from grace? Could it have been Gregory? Stepping out of his car, he slams the car door. It echoes around the lonely cemetery, making Gregory look up. Ashen faced, he mumbles something before scurrying off in the opposite direction. Ashley turns, smiles and waves, before marching to her car.

Atkins is just about to make a start towards the direction Matt Gregory has scurried off to when he feels a tap on his shoulder.

"Hey, you."

Glaring after him, a scowl on his face, Atkins turns around and his face drops. Because standing with a dozen white roses and tears in her eyes is Angela Marshall.

Bradd Chambers grew up on the outskirts of Derry~Londonderry in Northern Ireland. From a young age, he started reading and writing stories. He exceeded in English at school, and went on to obtain an NCTJ Diploma in Journalism at his local college, before graduating with a 2:1 in the same subject from Liverpool John Moores University. He has studied Creative Writing for years at colleges around the UK. He currently writes for several online magazines. Bradd's debut novel *'Someone Else's Life'* was released in June 2017, with the prequel novella, *'Our Jilly,'* following in November of the same year. *'In Too Deep,'* a book centring on suicide and mental health in his hometown was released in February 2019. He is currently working on a few stand-alones, with a few more based in his hometown of Derry and bringing back some familiar figures also in the pipeline.

"Thank you so much for taking the time to read my stories and helping to make my dream of becoming an author possible. If you enjoyed 'Daddy's Little Girl,' *or any other of my books, please don't forget to spread the word through word of mouth and/or social media. Also, a review on Amazon or Goodreads goes an awful long way, especially for Indie authors like myself who a lot of people haven't heard of."*

@braddchambers

Bradd Chambers

Daddy's Little Girl

Printed in Poland
by Amazon Fulfillment
Poland Sp. z o.o., Wrocław

53415024R00214